Claudine
at St Clare's

This is the fifth book
in the St Clare's school series

Dragon
Grafton Books
A Division of the Collins Publishing Group
8 Grafton Street, London W1X 3LA

Published by Dragon Books 1967
Reprinted 1968, 1969, 1970, 1971, 1972, 1973, 1974,
1975 (twice), 1976, 1977, 1978 (twice), 1979, 1980,
1981, 1982, 1983, 1984, 1985 (twice), 1986

First published in Great Britain by
Methuen & Co Ltd 1944

Copyright © Darrell Waters Ltd 1944

ISBN 0-583-30058-8

Printed and bound in Great Britain by
Collins, Glasgow

Set in Times

Enid Blyton

Claudine
at St Clare's

Text illustrations by Jenny Chapple

DRAGON
GRAFTON BOOKS
A Division of the Collins Publishing Group

LONDON GLASGOW
TORONTO SYDNEY AUCKLAND

Janet rummaged around in the drawers

Back at School Again

Pat and Isabel O'Sullivan walked into the fourth form-room at St. Clare's, and looked round.

"Fourth form," said Pat. "Golly, we're getting on, aren't we, Isabel!"

"Yes – fourth form seems a long way from the first form," said Isabel. "I say – do you remember when we were in the first form – ages ago? We were called the Stuck-up Twins then, because we hated St. Clare's, and didn't want to belong to it."

The twins thought back to the days when they had been first-formers. They remembered how they had settled down at St. Clare's, their first dislike of it turning to pride and admiration, and now here they were, fourth-formers at the beginning of the summer term!

"Don't the first-formers seem babies now?" said Pat. "We thought we were quite big when we first came, but when I see the first-formers now they seem very young to me! I shall enjoy being in the fourth form, won't you, Isabel?"

"I shall," said Isabel. "I hope we shall stay on at St. Clare's until we are in the top form – and I hope our friends do too."

"Well, some of them have left already," said Pat. "Pam isn't coming back, nor is Sheila. Lucy Oriell has gone too – to an Art School. She was going to stay on here, but she's too brilliant at her art, and she's won a scholarship to the best art school in the country."

"Good for Lucy!" said Isabel. "We shall miss her though. I wonder if there are any new girls this term?"

5

"Sure to be," said Pat. She looked round the big form-room. "I say, this is a fine room, isn't it? – the nicest classroom we've had so far. There's a wonderful view out of the window."

So there was. The twins could see miles of beautiful country. It was country they knew well now, and loved very much. Down below, in the school grounds, were the tennis-courts, the games fields, and the big swimming-pool. The girls could see the school gardens too, and the big kitchen garden full of fresh vegetables.

"Bags I sit by the window," said Pat. "Hallo, there's Bobby, and Janet!"

Roberta and Janet walked into the classroom, grinning. Bobby's freckled face had a very boyish look, and she was very like a boy in her ways, full of fun and tricks.

"Hallo!" she said. "Come to look at our new home? Nice room, isn't it?"

"What's our new form-mistress like?" said Pat. "Miss Ellis – she's supposed to be quite nice, isn't she?"

"Oh yes – very calm and unruffled and dignified," said Bobby. "She'll be all right."

"Got any new tricks to play, Janet?" asked Isabel. Janet always had a stock of tricks each term, most of them from her school-boy brother, who seemed to be a real scamp. Janet grinned.

"Wait and see," she said. "Anyway, I suppose I'd better go carefully now I'm a fourth-former. Can't rag about so much when you get high up the school. And I'm going to work for my matric. exam. too, so I guess I won't have much time for tricks."

"I guess you will, all the same," said Pat. "Any new girls, do you know?"

"Two or three," said Bobby. "Hallo, Hilary! Had good hols.?"

Hilary Wentworth came into the room, dark and

6

smiling. She had been at St. Clare's even longer than the twins.

"Hallo!" she said. "Yes, I had fine hols. I rode every day, and I played tennis on our hard court every day too. I say, who's the angel?"

"What do you mean?" asked the twins and Bobby.

"Oh, haven't you seen her?" said Hilary. "She's just arrived, complete with posh new trunk, three tennis rackets, and a handbag, with gold initials on. What do you bet your Cousin Alison will think she's one of the world's seven wonders? She's got pale golden hair, bobbed like angels in pictures, and a pointed face like a pixie, and a voice like a princess."

"Golly! Where is she?" said the others, with interest. "Will she be in our form?"

"She's down in the hall," said Hilary. "She arrived in the biggest car I've ever seen, with a crest on the panels, and two chauffeurs."

"Let's go and see her," said Pat. So the five of them went into the corridor, and hung over the stair banisters to see the newcomer.

She was still there – and it was quite true, she did look a bit like an angel, if an angel could be imagined dressed in school uniform, carrying three beautiful tennis rackets!

"She's lovely, isn't she?" said Bobby, who not being at all lovely herself, always admired beauty in others. "Yes – I bet Alison will follow her round like a dog. Alison isn't happy unless she's thinking some one is just too wonderful for words!"

Alison came up at that moment. She was the twins' cousin, a pretty, feather-headed little thing, with not many brains. "Hallo!" she said. "Did I hear you talking about me?"

"Yes," said Hilary. "We were just saying that you'd be sure to like that school-girl angel down there. Did you ever see anything like her?"

7

Alison leaned over the banisters – and, just as the others had guessed, she immediately lost her heart to the new girl.

"She looks like a princess from a fairy-tale," said Alison. "I'll go down and ask her if she wants to be shown round a bit."

Alison sped downstairs. The others grinned at one another. "Alison has lost her heart already," said Pat. "Poor old Alison – the wonderful friends she's made and lost! Do you remember Sadie, the American girl, and how Alison was for ever saying, 'Well, *Sadie* says so and so', and we made a song about it and sang it? Wasn't Alison cross?"

"Yes, and when she was in the second form she thought the drama mistress was simply wonderful, and when she was in the third form she lost her heart to the head-girl and made herself a perfect nuisance to her," said Janet. "Really, the times Alison has lost her heart to people, and they never think anything of her for it."

"Funny old feather-head," said Pat. "Look at her taking the angel's arm and going off with her, all over her already!"

"There's another new girl down there too," said Bobby. "She looks rather forlorn. Well, I do think Alison might take her round as well. Hie, Alison!"

But Alison had disappeared with the golden-haired angel. The twins went down the stairs and spoke to the other new girl.

"Hallo! You're new, aren't you? You'd better come and see Matron. We'll take you."

"What's your name?" said Pat, looking at the new girl, who was trying not to show that she felt new and lost.

"Pauline Bingham-Jones," said the new girl in rather an affected voice. "Yes, I'd be glad if you'd tell me what to do."

"Well, Matron is usually here to see to all the new

8

girls," said Hilary, a little puzzled. "I wonder where she is?"

"I haven't seen her at all," said Pat. "She wasn't here when we came, either."

"Funny," said Isabel. "Let's go to her room and find her. We've got to see her, anyway."

They went to Matron's room, taking Pauline with them. They banged on the door. They liked Matron, though they were very much in awe of her. She had been at St. Clare's for years and years, and some of the girls' mothers, who had also been at St. Clare's, had known her too.

A voice called out. "Come in!"

"That's not Matron's voice," said Pat, puzzled. She opened the door and went in, the others following. A woman in Matron's uniform sat sewing by the window. It wasn't the Matron they knew so well. The girls stared at her in surprise.

"Oh," said Pat. "We were looking for Matron."

"I am Matron this term," said the new Matron. "Your old Matron fell ill during the holidays, so I have come to take her place. I am sure we shall all get on very well together."

The girls stared at her. They didn't feel so sure about that. Their old Matron was fat and round and jolly, with a strong and comforting kind of face. This Matron was thin and sour-looking. She had very thin lips that met together in a straight line. She smiled at the girls, but her smile stayed at her mouth and did not reach her eyes.

"We came to find you," said Bobby. "Usually Matron meets the new girls. This is one of them. She has to give you her list of clothes and towels and things."

"I know that, thank you," said Matron, biting off the thread she was using. "Send all the new girls to me, will you? How many have arrived?"

9

The girls didn't know. They thought it was Matron's business to find out, not theirs. They thought of their old Matron, bustling about looking after the new-comers, making them welcome, taking them to their form-mistresses, or finding girls to take care of them.

"Well – this is Pauline Bingham-Jones," said Pat, at last. "There's another new girl somewhere. We saw her. Our Cousin Alison seems to be looking after her."

The girls disappeared from the room, leaving Pauline to the new Matron. They looked at one another and screwed up their noses. "Don't like her," said Isabel. "Looks like a bottle of vinegar!"

The others laughed. "I hope our old Matron will come back," said Bobby. "St. Clare's will seem funny without her. I wonder where Alison has gone with the angel."

Alison appeared at that moment, looking flushed and radiant. It was quite plain that she had made a friend already. With her was the "angel".

"Oh," said Alison, "Pat, Isabel, Bobby, Hilary – this is the Honourable Angela Favorleigh."

The Honourable Angela bent her head a little as if she was bowing to her subjects. Bobby grinned.

"I had a doll called Angela once," she said. "She was a bit like you! Well – I hope you'll like St. Clare's. Alison, take her to Matron."

"Where *is* Matron?" said Alison. "I've been looking for her."

"There's a new Matron this term," said Bobby. "You won't like her."

The Honourable Angela Favorleigh didn't like Bobby. She gazed at her as if she was something that smelt rather nasty. She turned to Alison and spoke in a pretty, high little voice.

"Well – let's go to Matron. I want to take my things off."

They went off together. Hilary laughed. "Well, we shall all know where Alison will be most of this term," she said, "In the Honourable's pocket!"

In the Fourth Form

"Look," said Bobby, "there's another new girl. She's got her things off, too. She looks as if she'd be a fourth-former, I should think."

The new girl came up, walking quickly as if she had somewhere to go. "Hallo," said Bobby. "You're new, aren't you? What form will you be in, do you know?"

"Fourth," said the girl. "My name's Eileen Paterson."

"We're fourth form too," said Pat, and she introduced herself and the others. "Do you want to be shown round a bit? Usually Matron is here to welcome people, but there is a new one this term who doesn't know the ropes yet."

The girl looked suddenly annoyed. "I know my way about, thank you," she said stiffly. "I've been here a week already."

Without saying any more she swung off. The others stared after her. "What's bitten *her*?" said Bobby. "No need to be rude like that. And what did she mean – that she's been here a week? Nobody comes back before the first day of term."

Mirabel came up, with her friend Gladys. "Hallo, hallo!" said the others. "Nice to see you again. I say, have you spoken to that girl who's just gone – new girl called Eileen Paterson. Seems to think the whole school belongs to her!"

"No, I haven't spoken to her yet," said Mirabel. "But

I know her mother is the Matron now – our old one is ill, you know. Eileen is the new Matron's daughter, and she's going to be educated here. She came with her mother a week ago, when her mother came to take over the job and see to the linen and things."

Bobby whistled. "Oh! No wonder she was annoyed when we said the new Matron ought to be welcoming the new girls, and didn't know the ropes yet!" she said. "And no wonder she knows her way about if she's already been here a week. I didn't like her much."

"Give her a chance," said Hilary. "You know how you feel sort of on the defensive when you come to anywhere new, and meet girls who've been here ages. You feel a kind of outsider at first."

There were new girls in the other, lower forms, but these did not interest the fourth-formers much. They were glad to see one another again – the twins, Bobby, Hilary, Kathleen, Doris, Carlotta, and the rest. They had all come up together into the fourth form. There were a few old girls left in the fourth form, most of whom the twins liked. Susan Howes was head of the form, a pleasant, kindly girl with a good sense of responsibility and fairness.

The fourth form settled down under Miss Ellis. She was firm and calm, seldom raised her voice, expected good work and saw that she got it. She was interested in the girls and fond of them, and they, in return, liked her very much.

The Honourable Angela Favorleigh looked more like an angel than ever in class, with her bobbed golden hair falling to her shoulders, the ends curling underneath most beautifully. All her school clothes, though cut to the same pattern as those of the others, were really beautiful.

"Do you know, she has every single pair of shoes especially made for her?" said Alison, in a hushed voice to the twins. "And she has a handbag to match every

12

single frock she wears, all with gold initials on."

"Shut up," said Pat. "Who cares about things like that? Your darling Angela is a snob."

"Well, why shouldn't she be?" said Alison, ready to defend her new friend at once. "Her family is one of the oldest in the country, she's got a third cousin who is a prince, and goodness knows how many titled relations!"

'You're a snob too, Alison," said Isabel, in disgust. "Why must you always suck up to people like that? Don't you know that it's what you *are* that matters, not what you have?"

"I'm not a snob", said Alison. "I'm pleased that Angela has chosen me for her friend, of course. I think she's lovely."

"Pity she hasn't got more brains," said Bobby. "Honestly, I don't believe she really knows her twelve times table!"

Angela Favorleigh certainly was a snob. She was intensely proud of her family, of its wealth, its cars, and her own well-bred looks. She was very particular about making friends. She liked Alison because the girl was pretty and dainty, had beautiful manners and quite plainly adored the lovely Angela from the bottom of her foolish little heart.

Angela liked very few of her form. Bobby she detested because she had said she was like a doll. Carlotta she would have nothing to do with at all.

Carlotta didn't mind in the least. The dark-eyed, dark-haired girl had once been a little circus-girl, and she was not at all ashamed of it. Her mother had been a circus-rider, but her father was a gentleman, and now Carlotta lived with her father and grandmother in the holidays, for her mother was dead. She had learnt to be lady-like, to have good manners, and was very popular indeed – but she had never forgotten the exciting days of the circus, and she often amused the others by turning cart-wheels, or going completely mad in a foreign,

Spanish way that the girls enjoyed very much.

Alison had told Angela the histories of all the girls, Carlotta included, and Angela had turned up her delicate little nose when she heard that Carlotta had actually ridden horses in a circus.

"How *can* they have her here, in a school like this?" she said. "I am sure my people wouldn't have sent me here if they had known that."

"Why did you come to St. Clare's?" asked Alison, curiously. "It's supposed to be a sensible, no-nonsense school, you know – not a swanky one."

"I didn't want to come," said Angela. "My mother wanted to send me to a much nicer school, but my father has funny ideas. He said I wanted my corners rubbed off."

"Oh, Angela! You haven't any corners!" said Alison. "Honestly, I don't think you've any faults at all."

This was the kind of thing that Angela loved hearing, and was one reason why she liked Alison for a friend. She looked at Alison out of innocent blue eyes, and smiled an angelic smile.

"You do say nice things, Alison," she said. "You are far and away the nicest girl in the form. I can't bear that common Eileen, nor that awful Carlotta, nor that dreadful Pauline Bingham-Jones."

Pauline certainly wasn't much of a success. In her way she seemed as much of a snob as Angela, but she could not carry it off so well, because her clothes were not beautifully made, and she had no marvellous possessions such as Angela had. But she too turned up her nose at Carlotta, and disliked the ready-witted Bobby. As for Eileen, she would hardly speak to her at all.

"I don't see why Eileen should be allowed to join the school just because her mother is here as Matron," said Pauline, in her rather affected voice. "Good gracious me – we shall have the cook's daughter here next, and

14

the gardener's too! It's bad enough to have Carlotta. She always looks so wild and don't-carish."

Carlotta always did look a little wild at the beginning of term, partly because she was no longer under the rather strict eye of her grandmother. But nobody minded Carlotta's untidiness and wildness. It was all part of the vivacious, amusing girl. Carlotta knew that Angela and Pauline didn't like her, and she took a real pleasure in talking slang, making rude faces, and unexpectedly walking on her hands in front of them.

Miss Ellis, however, did not encourage things of this sort in the fourth form. Her form was a kind of half-way house, where girls had to learn to shed their irresponsible ways, and to become more serious, reliable members of the school. As soon as they moved up into the fifth and sixth, they had studies of their own, instead of common rooms, and were expected to take a good deal of responsibility.

So Carlotta was often called to order by Miss Ellis, in her low, firm voice, and then Angela and Pauline looked down their noses at the one-time circus-girl, and whispered mocking things to the girl next to them.

Pauline and Angela vied with each other in their boasting. The girls sometimes giggled to hear them.

"My third cousin – the one who is a prince," Angela would say, "he has an aeroplane of his own, and has promised to take me up in it."

"Haven't you *been* up in an aeroplane yet?" Pauline would say, with affected surprise. "Good gracious! I've been up three times already. That was when I was staying with the Lacy-Wrights. Fancy, they had sixteen bathrooms in their house – well, it was really a mansion, of course. . . ."

"I bet you haven't more than one bathroom in your own home," said Angela, spitefully. "We've got seven."

"We've got nine, if you count the two in the servants' quarters," said Pauline, at once. The other girls stared

15

at her in surprise. They could well believe that Angela had scores of bathrooms, for wealth was written all over the little snob – but somehow Pauline didn't fit in with a number of bathrooms, a fleet of expensive cars and things like that.

"Well," said Bobby, "let me count *my* bathrooms. Three for myself – four for Mother – five for Daddy – two for visitors – er, how many's that?"

"Idiot!" said Pat, giggling. Angela and Pauline scowled.

"I can't remember whether we've got a bathroom at home or not," said Hilary, entering into the fun. "Let me think hard!"

But no amount of teasing would make either Angela or Pauline stop their vieing with each other. If it wasn't bathrooms, it was cars; if it wasn't cars, it was their beautiful, expensively-dressed mothers; if it wasn't mothers, it was clothes. The others really got very tired of it.

Eileen Paterson did not seem to mind very much being cold-shouldered by Angela and Pauline. She only spoke with eagerness of one thing – her elder brother. He was at work somewhere in the next big town, and it was quite plain that Eileen adored him.

"His name is Edgar," she said. "We call him Eddie."

"You would," said Angela, cattily. "And if he was called Alfred, you'd call him Alf. And if he was called Herbert, you'd call him Herb – or Erb perhaps."

Eileen flushed. "You're a beast, Angela," she said. "You wait till you see Eddie – Edgar, I mean. He's marvellous! His hair's curly, and he's got the loveliest smile. He's the best brother in the world. He's working terribly hard at his job. You see, Mother lost a lot of money, so that's why she had to take a job as Matron, and why Eddie – Edgar – had to go to work."

"Your family history doesn't interest me, Eileen,"

16

said Angela, coldly, and went off with Alison. Eileen shrugged her shoulders.

"Little snob!" she said, loudly. "She wants a good spanking."

Carlotta agreed with her. "Yes – sometimes my hand tingles because it wants to slap Angela hard," she said. "But now I'm a fourth-former – what a pity! I shall quite forget how to give a slap to any one who needs it!"

"Oh no you won't," said Bobby, laughing at the solemn Carlotta. "When you fly into a temper, you'll forget all about being a fourth-former – you'll just be the same wild Carlotta you've always been!"

The Arrival of Claudine

Before a week had gone by, a fourth new girl arrived. Mam'zelle herself announced her coming.

"I have a surprise for you," she beamed one morning, coming in to give a French lesson. "We shall soon have another companion in the fourth form. She arrived to-day."

"Why is she so late in coming?" asked Pat, in surprise.

"She has just recovered from the measle," said Mam'zelle, who always spoke of this illness in the singular and not in the plural. "The measle is a most tiresome disease. Claudine had a very bad measle, and she could not come back any sooner."

"Claudine?" said Isabel. "What a pretty name! I like it."

"Ah, and you will like the little Claudine too!" said

17

Mam'zelle. "For she is French. She is my niece!"

This was news to the girls. They hadn't even known that Mam'zelle had a niece. One coming to St. Clare's too!

"I hope she will be happy at St. Clare's," said Hilary, feeling that some one ought to say the right thing.

"Ah, she will be very happy," said Mam'zelle. "She would be happy anywhere, the little Claudine. There never was such a child for happiness. Always she smiles and laughs, and always she plays the trick and the joke."

This sounded good. The girls began to look forward to Claudine's coming. They looked at Mam'zelle expectantly, hoping to hear more.

Then Mam'zelle's face grew solemn. She pinched her glasses more firmly on her nose and gazed at the listening girls with her short-sighted, much-magnified eyes.

"I have especially asked for Claudine to come here," she said. "Before, she has been to a Convent School, but it was too strict for her, and always they found fault with the poor little Claudine. They said she cared nothing for any one, nor for any rules or customs. And I thought to myself, 'Ah, the good, hard-working Bobby was once like that – and see what St. Clare's has done for her! Now she works for her Matric. and she is as good as gold! Maybe the same thing will happen to my little Claudine.' "

Bobby looked uncomfortable as Mam'zelle made this speech. She wasn't at all sure that she wanted to be referred to as 'good as gold'. But Mam'zelle was so much in earnest that Bobby made no protest. It wouldn't have been any good, anyway! Mam'zelle swept on with her speech.

"And so the little Claudine comes today, well-recovered from the measle, and you will give her a grand welcome, will you not? For your old Mam'zelle's sake?"

18

"Of course we'll make her welcome," said Susan Howes, and most of the others murmured the same, except Angela, Alison and Pauline, who all put on a bored look, as if a niece belonging to Mam'zelle wasn't worth giving a thought to.

"Ah, you are good kind girls," said Mam'zelle. "I will introduce Claudine to you as soon as she comes. She will love you all. She is a good girl though she seems to care nothing for what is good and proper. But you will change all that, *n'est-ce pas*?"

The girls thought that Claudine sounded distinctly amusing. It would be fun to have a French girl in the class! They glanced at one another, thinking that of all the new girls, this latest one sounded the most promising.

About five minutes before the lesson finished the door was opened, and a strange girl appeared. She was small, dark and smart. She had a very cheeky look and she gave a quick sidelong glance at the girls before advancing to Mam'zelle.

Mam'zelle gave a shriek, and then flung herself on the new girl. She kissed her several times on both cheeks, she stroked her dark hair, and poured out such a torrent of French that no one could follow it.

The girl replied in smooth, polite French, and kissed Mam'zelle on each cheek. She did not seem to mind her aunt's outburst in the least.

"Ah, ma petite Claudine, here you are at last!" cried Mam'zelle. She swung the girl round to face the class. "Now see, here is the little Claudine," said Mam'zelle, her glasses falling off her nose in her violent delight. "Greet your new friends, Claudine."

"Hallo, buddies!" said Claudine, amiably. The girls stared in surprise and then giggled. It was funny to hear such an American expression from the little French girl.

"What did you say?" said Mam'zelle, who was not

well up in American slang. "Did you say 'Hello, bodies'? That is not correct, Claudine. You should say 'Hallo, everybody.'"

The class roared. Claudine grinned. Mam'zelle beamed. She was plainly very proud of Claudine and very fond of her.

The bell rang for the end of class. Mam'zelle picked out Hilary. "Hilary, you will take the little Claudine with you, please, and show her everything. She will feel strange and shy, poor little one."

Mam'zelle was quite mistaken about that, however. Claudine didn't feel shy, and certainly didn't seem to feel strange. In fact she acted as if she had known the girls all her life! She spoke easily and naturally to them. Her English was good, though like Mam'zelle, she sometimes put things in an unusual way.

She had been to school in France, and then had spent a term or two at a Convent School in England. It seemed that Claudine did not want to remain at her last school and they did not want to keep her.

"You see – it was most unfortunate – the Science Mistress went up a ladder into a tree to collect some curious fungus that grew there," explained Claudine, in her little French voice. "And I came along and borrowed the ladder. So we did not have a Science lesson that day."

"Golly! Do you mean to say that you left the teacher stranded up the tree?" said Bobby. "Well, you have got a nerve! No wonder Mam'zelle thinks St. Clare's will be good for you. You can't do that sort of thing here."

"No?" said Claudine. "What a pity. Still, maybe you have good fun. I am sorry I did not come back to school on the first day. But I had caught a measle."

The girls giggled. Every one liked Claudine, except Angela. Even Pauline listened to the new girl, and Alison was much amused by her. But Angela as usual looked down her nose.

"What did I tell you?" she said to Alison. "First we have to have Matron's daughter, and now we have to have Mam'zelle's niece! I can't see what you find to be amused at in Claudine, Alison. I'm surprised at you."

"Well, I like her voice and her manners," said Alison. "I like the way she uses her hands when she talks – just like Mam'zelle does. She's really quite amusing, Angela."

Angela did not like Alison to disagree with her about anything. She looked coldly at her friend and then turned away sulkily. That was always the way she punished any one – but withdrawing from them and sulking. Alison couldn't bear it.

Alison tried to make it up. She went after Angela, and took her hand. She praised her and flattered her, and at last Angela condescended to smile again on her willing slave.

Then Alison was happy. "You needn't think I shall bother about Claudine at all," she said to Angela. "She's a common little thing, really."

"Not so common as Carlotta," said Angela, spitefully. Alison looked uncomfortable. She sincerely liked Carlotta, who was absolutely honest, truthful and straight, besides being amusing company. Even her hot temper was likeable. Alison thought that Carlotta was more completely herself, more natural than any of the other girls. And to be natural was to be very likeable.

Claudine settled in at once. She took a desk at the back of the room, and bagged a locker in the common room. She arranged her belongings in the locker, and put a photograph of her mother on top. She had brought a fine big cake with her and shared it generously all round, though Angela refused a slice. Alison did too, after hesitating. She was afraid that Angela might go into a sulk again if she saw her sharing the cake.

21

At first the girls were very much amused with Claudine, but they soon discovered that she had very un-English ways. For instance, she thought nothing of copying from someone else's book! She had a quick brain, but she was often lazy – and then she would simply copy the answers set down by the girl next to her. This was Mirabel, whose brains were not of the highest order. So, more often than not, Claudine copied down mistakes. But she did not seem to mind at all.

"Look here – we oughtn't to let Claudine cheat like this," said Pat. "She keeps *on* copying from Mirabel. Mirabel says Claudine didn't bother to do a single sum – she copied the answers of all hers!"

"The funny thing is, she does it so openly," said Isabel. "I mean – I really don't believe she thinks it's wrong!"

Claudine was very astonished when Susan Howes, the head girl of the form, spoke to her about the copying.

"It's cheating, Claudine; surely you can see that!" said Susan, her honest face glowing scarlet, for she did not like accusing any one of cheating.

"No, I do not see it at all," said Claudine. "You all see me do it. Cheating is a secret thing."

"No, it isn't," said Susan. "Cheating is cheating whether you do it in front of any one, or on the sly. Besides, it's so silly of you to copy from Mirabel. She gets so many answers wrong. Miss Ellis will find out and then you'll get into a row."

"You think then it would be better to copy from Hilary?" asked Claudine, seriously. Susan sighed.

"Claudine, you mustn't copy from *any* one. I know French people have different ideas from ours – Mam'zelle has, for instance – but you'll have to try and get into our ways if you're going to be happy here."

"I am happy anywhere," said Claudine at once. "Well,

Susan, I will perhaps not copy again – only if I have not done any of my prep at all."

Another thing that the girls found irritating about Claudine was the way she borrowed things. She borrowed pencils, rubbers, rulers, books – anything she happened to want at the moment. And nine times out of ten she didn't give them back.

"I forget," she explained. "I borrow a pencil and I use it, and I am most grateful for it – and then I forget about it, and poor Hilary, she says, 'Where is my pencil, I have lost my pencil' – and there it is on my desk all the time, not at all lost."

"Well, you might *try* and remember to give back things you borrow," said Hilary. "After all, it was a silver pencil of mine you borrowed, one I like very much. And you might ask permission before you borrow things."

"Oh, you English!" sighed Claudine. "Well, I will be good, and always I will say 'Dear Hilary, please, please lend me your so-beautiful silver pencil.'"

Hilary laughed. No one could help being amused by Claudine. She rolled her expressive black eyes round and used her hands in the same way that Mam'zelle did. After all, she hadn't been in England very long – she would learn English ways before the term was over!

Beware of Matron!

The first few weeks passed, and soon the fourth-formers, those who had come up from the third form, felt as if they had always been in the fourth form! They looked down on the third-formers, and as for the second- and first-form girls, well, they were very small fry indeed. No fourth-former would have dreamed of taking any notice of them.

The summer term was always a nice one. There was tennis, and there was swimming. Angela proved to be an unexpectedly good swimmer, deft and swift. Alison, who disliked the water, did her best to shine in it in order to try and keep up with her beloved Angela.

Claudine frankly hated the water. She entirely refused to go in, much to the games-mistress's annoyance.

"Claudine! What is the use of coming to an English school if you do not learn the good things in it?" she said.

"Swimming is not a good thing," said Claudine. "It is a horrible thing, wet and cold and shivery. And I do not like your habit of playing so many games. Tennis is also silly."

As no one could undress Claudine by force, she did not go into the water. The others teased her by splashing her as much as they could. The games-mistress saw that sooner or later Claudine would be pushed in, fully-dressed, and she sent her back to the school.

Claudine's tennis was even worse than Carlotta's. Carlotta had never managed to play properly. She was still very wild and uncontrolled in games, and the tennis ball was quite as likely to drop into the middle of the distant swimming-pool as over the tennis net! But Claudine did not even attempt to hit the ball!

"This is a so-silly game," she would say, and put down her racket and go off by herself.

"But Claudine, it's your tennis-practice time. You *must* come," Hilary would say.

"I must not," was Claudine's reply, and that was that.

Angela played a neat and deft game. She always brought her three beautiful rackets out with her, in spite of every one's teasing. Pauline was jealous of them. She tried to pay Angela out by being spiteful.

"I've two or three more rackets at home," she said in a loud voice. "But it isn't good manners to bring more than one to school. My mother says that would be showing off. No well-bred person shows off."

Nobody liked Angela's conceit, but nobody liked Pauline's spite, either. In fact, few people liked Pauline for, rich and grand as she made out her people and her home to be, she was a plain and unattractive girl – unlike Angela, who was really lovely. Nobody could help looking at the angel-faced Angela without admiration and pleasure. Alison thought she was the prettiest girl she had ever seen.

Eileen was moderately good at both tennis and swimming. She was moderately good at her lessons too. She took a liking to Alison, for some reason or other, and was very upset when Alison showed her far too plainly that she had no time for her.

"*Why* can't you sometimes walk with me when we go out in the afternoons?" Eileen said to Alison. "You can't *always* walk with Angela. And *why* do you always refuse when I offer you sweets? They won't poison you!"

"I know," said Alison, coldly. "I just don't want them, that's all. And I don't particularly want to walk with you, either."

"I suppose Angela told you not to!" said Eileen, angrily. "You haven't got any mind of your own, have you? Whatever Angela thinks, *you* think! Whatever Angela does, *you* do! You're even trying to grow your hair the way she grows hers – down to your shoulders and curled under. Well, you look a perfect fright like that!"

Alison was very offended. She looked coldly at Eileen.

"Well, if you want to know, Angela doesn't approve of you, and as she is my friend, I respect her wishes.

25

Anyway, I don't approve of you, either. You're a tell-tale!"

Eileen walked away, her face scarlet with rage. Alison's last hit had gone home. Eileen ran to her mother with tales, and there was nothing the fourth form did that the new Matron did not know about.

Worse than that, if Eileen told her mother that some one had been horrid to her, the Matron soon saw to it that that some one was called to her room, and shown a huge rent in one of her bed-sheets to mend, or holes in her games stockings, or buttons off vests.

"I believe she makes the holes on purpose and pulls the buttons off herself!" raged Angela, who had been given three stockings to darn in her spare-time. "I've never darned a stocking in my life. What's a matron for if she doesn't keep our things mended?"

"Well, it is the rule at St. Clare's that we do some of our own mending," said Pat. "But I must say, Angela, I can't think that you made all those enormous holes in your stockings! I've never seen you with a hole yet."

"Oh, I know I didn't make them," said Angela, trying in vain to thread a needle with wool. "*How* do you make the wool go through the needle's eye? I've been trying to thread this for ages."

The girls laughed. Angela had no idea how to double over the end of the wool and thread the darning-needle in the right way. Alison took the needle and stocking away from her.

"I'll do your darning, Angela," she said. "Don't worry. I bet it's that tell-tale Eileen that ran to her mother about something you said or did – and so Matron gave you this work to do out of spite."

Alison darned the three stockings – not very well, it is true, because darning was not one of Alison's gifts. But Angela was grateful, and was so sweet to Alison that the girl was in the seventh heaven of delight.

Pauline was the next to get into trouble with Matron.

She, like Angela, turned up her nose at Eileen, and would have no more to do with her than she could help. When she told Bobby one morning that she had a sore throat, Eileen overheard. She went off out of the room, and in a short while Pauline was sent for.

"I hear you have a sore throat, Pauline," said Matron, with a thin-lipped smile. "You should report to me at once. Eileen felt worried about you, and told me. It was very kind of her. I have a gargle for you here, and some medicine."

"Oh, my throat is much better now," said Pauline in alarm. And it was – but Matron was not going to let her off. She made poor Pauline gargle for ten minutes with a horrible concoction, and then gave her some equally nasty medicine to drink.

Pauline went back to the others, angry and afraid. She glanced round the room to make sure that Eileen was not there.

"Eileen's been telling tales again," she said. "She told her mother I'd got a sore throat – and I've just been having an awful time. I feel quite sick. I know Eileen told Matron she didn't like me, and that's why Matron gave me such a beastly time."

"We'll have to be careful what we say and do to Eileen," said Alison, scared, for she hated medicine of any sort. "Perhaps we'd better be friendlier."

"I shall not be friendlier," said Claudine. "That is a girl I do not like."

And, far from being friendlier, Claudine really seemed to go out of her way to be rude to Eileen! The result was that Matron came down heavily on Claudine, and gave her a whole basketful of mending to do!

"You have torn the hem of both your sheets," she told Claudine. "And you have holes in all your stockings, and you need a patch in one of your vests. You are a very naughty, careless girl. You will do most of this mending yourself, as a punishment."

27

Claudine said nothing. She took the basket of mending and put it on top of her locker. At first the girls thought she would simply forget all about it, and refuse to do it, as she refused to do other things. But, to their surprise, Claudine took down the mending and settled herself in a corner of the common room to do it.

Bobby watched her needle flying in and out. "I say – you do sew beautifully!" she said. "You really do! And your darning is as good as embroidery. It's beautiful."

"I like sewing and darning," said Claudine. "We are always taught that well in France. You English girls are clumsy with your needles. You can bang all kinds of silly balls about, but you cannot make a beautiful darn!"

"Claudine, put that mending away now, and come out and swim," said Susan. "It's such a nice sunny day."

But nice sunny days did not appeal to Claudine at all. "I can see the sun out of the window," she said, sewing away hard. "Leave me. I like sewing."

Bobby stared hard at the bent head of the little French girl. Then she gave a chuckle.

"Claudine, you like sewing a whole lot better than you like swimming and games, don't you?" she said.

"Yes," said Claudine. "Sewing is very okay, I think."

The others laughed. Claudine always sounded funny when she brought American slang into her speech.

"I believe this is all a little trick of Claudine's," said Bobby. "She wants to have a real excuse for getting out of games! We all know we have to give up games time if we have mending to do – and Claudine has made Matron give her a punishment that will get her out of games, and give her something to do instead that she really likes!"

Miss Ellis came into the room. "Hurry up and go out, girls," she said. "Don't waste a minute of this nice fine day. Claudine, put away your sewing."

"I'm sorry, Miss Ellis, but Matron said I was to do

28

my darning and mending before I could go to play with the others," said Claudine, looking up with big innocent dark eyes. "It is very sad – but I suppose I must do this, Miss Ellis?"

"Hmm," said Miss Ellis, not at all taken in by the wide-open eyes. "I'll have a word with Matron."

But Matron was quite insistent that Claudine had been careless, and must mend her things, so Miss Ellis left the girl to her sewing. And Claudine had a very nice time, sewing away happily in a corner of the sunny room, hearing the shouts of the girls in the swimming-pool. She had no wish whatever to join them!

"Horrible wet cold water!" she thought to herself, and then looked up as she heard footsteps coming into the room. It was her aunt, Mam'zelle.

"Ah, *ma petite*!" said Mam'zelle, beaming. "So you are here. Let me see your sewing. It is beautiful! Why cannot these English girls sew? Where are the others?"

"In the water," said Claudine, in French. "Always they are in the water, or hitting a ball, these English girls. Me, I prefer to sew, *ma tante*!"

"Quite right, little Claudine!" said Mam'zelle, who, for all her years in England had never been able to understand why English girls liked cold water, hitting balls, and running madly about. "You are happy, my little one?"

"Yes, thank you, *ma tante*," answered Claudine demurely. "But I am a little dull. Does nothing ever happen in these English schools?"

"Nothing," said Mam'zelle. But she was wrong. Things did happen – and they were just about to!

Angela Gets a Surprise

About the third week of the term, when every one had settled down, and got into their work, Angela had a surprise.

She had been playing tennis, and one of the balls had been lost. "Don't let's bother to look for it now," said Bobby, who hated to stop in the middle of a game. "It's sure to turn up. Tennis balls always do. If it doesn't we'll look for it afterwards."

The ball hadn't turned up, and Angela had offered to look for it. The others had music-lessons to go to, or elocution practice. Angela was the only one free.

"All right," said Hilary. "Thanks, Angela. You look for the ball, and pop it back into the box with the others if you find it."

The other three girls ran back to the school, and Angela began to look for the lost ball. It was nowhere to be seen. The court they had been playing on backed on to a high wall, and Angela wondered if the ball could possibly have gone over it.

"I remember Bobby sending a pretty high ball once," she thought to herself. "Well, it doesn't seem to be *this* side of the wall – so I'll just slip out of the garden gate here and look in the lane."

The girl opened the gate and went out into the narrow green lane. She looked about for the ball, and at last saw it. As she went to get it, she gave a start of surprise. A tall, rather thin youth was behind the bush near the ball.

Angela picked up the ball and was about to go back into the school grounds when the boy spoke to her.

"I say – do you belong to St. Clare's?"

Angela looked at him and didn't like him. He had hair that was curly, and much too long. His eyes were small and puffy underneath, and he was very pale.

"What business is it of yours whether I belong to St. Clare's or not?" said Angela, in her haughtiest voice.

"Now look here – don't go all stuffy and stupid," said the boy, coming out from behind the bush. "I just want a word with you."

"Well, I don't want a word with *you*," said Angela, and she opened the garden gate. The boy tried to stop her going through.

"Wait a bit," he said, and his voice sounded so urgent that Angela turned round in surprise. "I want you to take a message to one of the girls for me," he said.

"Of course I shan't do that," said Angela. "Let me pass, please. You deserve to be reported for this."

"Listen. You tell Eileen that Eddie wants to see her," said the boy. "Wait – I've got a note for her. Will you give it to her?"

"Oh – so you're Eileen's brother, are you?" said Angela. "All right – I'll give her the note. But I can't think why you don't come right in and see your mother and Eileen too, if you want to. Your mother is Matron here, isn't she?"

"Yes," said Eddie. "But for goodness' sake don't go and tell my mother you've seen me. She doesn't know I'm here. I'd get into an awful row with her if she knew I was."

"Your mother gets lots of people into rows beside you!" said Angela, taking the note.

The girl went through the gate and shut it. Then she stuffed the note into the pocket of her blazer, meaning to give it to Eileen when she saw her.

Eileen was not about when Angela went back to the

31

The boy tried to stop Angela

cloakroom to change her shoes. The girl saw Alison there and began to tell her what had happened.

"I say, Alison!" she said, "A funny thing happened just now. I went out into the lane to look for a tennis ball, and there was a boy there, hiding."

"Gracious!" said Alison, startled. "What did you do?"

"He was an awful creature," said Angela, beginning to exaggerate, as she usually did when she had a tale to tell. "Honestly, he looked like the boy who brings the fish here every day – you know, that awful boy with the too-long hair and the piercing whistle! I half expected him to say 'I've brought the 'addock and 'ake and 'alibut, miss!' like the fish-boy said to Matron the other day, thinking she was the cook."

Alison laughed. So did one or two other girls in the cloakroom. Angela loved an admiring audience. She went on with her tale, not seeing that Eileen had come in to put away gym. shoes.

"Well, he asked me if I belonged to St. Clare's, and I put him properly in his place, you may be sure! And then he told me who he was. You'll never guess!"

The girls crowded round her in interest. "Who?" said Alison. "How should we know who it was?"

"Well, it was dear, darling wonderful Eddie, Eileen's big brother!" said Angela. "As common as could be! I nearly asked him why he didn't get his hair cut!"

Some one elbowed her way roughly through the group round Angela. It was Eileen, her cheeks scarlet. She glared at Angela.

"You frightful fibber!" she said. "My brother's nowhere near St. Clare's! How dare you make up a story like that – I shall go and tell my mother at once – you hateful, horrid little snob!"

She burst into tears and went out of the door. The girls stared after her.

"I say!" said Alison, "she really *will* go to Matron –

and there's sure to be a row. You didn't make it up, did you, Angela?"

Angela raised her voice and shouted after Eileen. "Well, go and tell if you like – but your darling Eddie begged and begged me *not* to let your mother know he was here. So you are just as likely to get *him* into a row, as me!"

Eileen turned round, looking scared. It was plain that she now believed what Angela said. It *had* been Eddie!

"What did he say to you?" she asked Angela, in a strangled voice. "Did he want to see me?"

"Shan't tell you," said Angela, in an irritating voice. "I *was* going to do you a good turn and give you his message – but if you behave like this I'm jolly well not going to be a go-between for you and dear, darling Eddie!"

Just at that very thrilling moment Miss Ellis put her head in at the door, looking most annoyed.

"Girls! Didn't you hear the bell? What in the world are you doing, chattering here in the cloakroom? You know that isn't allowed. Really, I do wish you fourth-formers would realize that you are half-way up the school and not in the first form! I am most annoyed at having to come and fetch you."

"Sorry, Miss Ellis," said every one, and hurried to go out of the cloakroom back to the classroom, where they had prep to do. Certainly they had heard the bell – but who could tear themselves away when a first-class quarrel was going on between the angelic Angela, and the unpopular Eileen?

Angela felt delighted when she sat down at her desk. Now she had Eileen exactly where she wanted her – under her thumb! And if Eileen ever told tales of her again and got Matron to give her heaps of mending to do, she, Angela, would threaten to tell Matron about dear Eddie! Angela smiled a secret smile to herself, which made her look more like an angel than ever. It

34

was extraordinary how Angela could look so innocently beautiful when she was thinking spiteful thoughts!

Eileen saw the secret smile. She pursed her lips together and ground her teeth. She hated Angela bitterly in that moment, with as deep a hatred as the love she had for Eddie. How dared Angela call Eddie common? How dared she say he was like that horrid little fishmonger's boy, with his long, greasy hair and shrill whistle?

To Eileen her brother Edgar was the most wonderful being in the world. Their father had died when they were both very young, and their mother was a hard and stern woman. The little girl had turned to her big brother for love and companionship, and the boy had guarded and cherished his sister tenderly.

"As soon as I grow up, I'll get a fine job, and make heaps of money for you and Mother," he told Eileen. "Then Mother won't need to work so hard and be so tired and cross, and you shall have lots of nice presents. You'll see what wonderful things I'll do!"

And now Angela had poured scorn on to darling, kind Eddie. Eileen felt as if she must burst with anger and tears. She was very anxious too. Why had Eddie left Woolaton, where he worked, and come to see her secretly? What had happened? Oh, if only that beast of an Angela would tell her!

Eileen thought of Eddie out there in the lane. She had not seen him for some weeks, and she was longing to talk to him and tell him everything. Perhaps he felt the same and had got some time off to slip along and see her. Perhaps he didn't want to come up to the school, because then he would have to see Mother too, and that would spoil the heart-to-heart talk they might have together.

Eileen looked at Angela. The girl was studying her French book, looking serene and lovely. Eileen gritted her teeth again, knowing that she would soon have to do something very difficult, something she would hate, and which yet would have to be done gracefully.

"I'll have to go and beg Angela's pardon and ask her to tell me what Eddie said," thought Eileen. "Beast! I do hate her!"

She gave a loud sigh. Miss Ellis looked up. She had already seen that Eileen was making no attempt at all to do her prep.

"Eileen, don't you feel well?" she inquired. "As far as I can see you haven't done any work at all."

"I'm all right, thank you, Miss Ellis," said Eileen hurriedly. "This – this French is a bit difficult today, that's all."

"I should think it must be *very* difficult to learn your French out of your geography book," said Miss Ellis in her calm voice. Eileen looked hurriedly down at her book – dash – it was her geography book she was holding! Trust the sharp eyes of Miss Ellis to spot that!

She said nothing, but got out her French book. Angela looked round and gave a scornful little smile. She knew quite well why it was that Eileen muddled her books just then – she was worried about dear darling Eddie. Well – let her worry!

Alison sat next to Eileen, and she couldn't help feeling a little sorry for her. Although she was such a little scatter-brain, Alison was sensitive to the feelings of others, and she knew that Eileen was desperately longing to know about Eddie. So, after prep was over she went to Angela and spoke to her.

"I say, Angela – hadn't you better tell Eileen her brother's message? She's in an awful state. She sighed so hard in prep that she almost blew my papers off the desk!"

Angela was not amused at Alison's feeble little joke, neither did she like her giving her advice of any sort. She turned away, and Alison's heart sank. Now Angela was going to go all cold and sulky again. The beautiful

36

little face was hard and haughty, and Alison knew it
would be ages before she could get a smile out of her
again.

She was just going after her when Eileen came up,
a forced smile on her face. "Angela! Can I speak to you
for a minute? Alone, please?"

Angela and Eileen

"I'm busy," said Angela, curtly.

"No, you're not," said Eileen, trying to speak calmly
and smilingly. "It's important, Angela."

"I hope you're going to apologize for your rudeness
to me," said Angela, haughtily. "I certainly shan't speak
to you unless you do. I'm not going to let people like
you call me a hateful horrid snob."

Eileen swallowed hard and forced herself to speak,
though the words almost choked her.

"I beg your pardon, Angela. I – I lost my temper!"

Carlotta overheard this conversation and unexpectedly came to Eileen's help. "Well, if you ask *my*
opinion I think Angela ought to apologize to *you*,
Eileen, for some of *her* remarks!" said Carlotta, in her
fresh, candid voice. "I'm jolly certain I wouldn't apologize to *her* – little cat!"

Angela turned on Carlotta in a fury, her blue eyes
gleaming with spite.

"You don't suppose we care what circus-folk think
do you?" she said. But instead of being crushed,
Carlotta gave one of her hearty laughs.

"If I wasn't in the fourth form I'd give you the
hardest slap you've ever had in your life, Angela," she

37

said, amiably. "A good spanking would be the best thing you could have."

"Nobody has ever laid a finger on me in my life," said Angela, feeling an intense desire to smack Carlotta's vivid little face.

"I can tell that," said Carlotta. "You'd be a lot nicer if they had. Come on, Eileen, leave Angela to her haughty ways and come and play cards with me in the common room."

Eileen felt very grateful to Carlotta for her unexpected help but she shook her head. She had simply got to find out about Eddie. How unfortunate it was that it should be Angela, of all people, that he had spoken to. Any of the others would have been decent about it – except Pauline perhaps.

Carlotta shrugged her shoulders and went off to find Bobby and the twins. She didn't like Eileen very much, because she thought, as the others did, that she was a tell-tale – but all the same Angela was behaving like a little cat to her, putting out those claws of hers and giving as deep a scratch as she could!

Angela turned to Eileen. "Well," she said, "you've apologized and I accept your apology. What do you want to say to me?"

"Angela, *please* tell me what Eddie said," begged Eileen. "Did he give you a message for me?"

"Yes. He gave me a letter," said Angela. Eileen went red with excitement and stared at Angela eagerly.

"Please give it to me," she said.

"I don't see why I should," said Angela. "I don't think I *ought* to take notes and deliver them, like this."

Eileen knew that Angela was saying this to irritate her. She felt intensely angry, but she kept her temper.

"You'll never have to do it again," she said. "I'll tell Edgar he mustn't send in notes this way. He must post a letter. Please give me the note."

"Now, listen," said Angela, suddenly getting down to

38

business, "if I give you this note and don't tell your mother I saw her precious Eddie, you've got to promise *me* something."

"What?" asked Eileen, in surprise. "I'll promise you anything!"

"All right," said Angela. "You've jolly well got to promise me that you'll never run sneaking to your mother about *me*, see? I'm not going to have shoals of mending to do any more – I hate sewing and darning! I know you complained to Matron about me before, and that's why she presented me with stockings that had holes in *I* never made!"

"You're not to say things like that about my mother," said Eileen.

"Well, I shall," said Angela. "We all know you sneak to her about us. Sneak about the others all you like – but don't you sneak about *me* any more. You'll be sorry if you do."

There was nothing for it but to promise. So Eileen promised. "I won't sneak about you," she said in a trembling voice. "I don't sneak. If Mother hands out sewing and mending, it's not my fault."

"Hmm," said Angela, disbelievingly, "well, all I can says is – it's a funny thing that as soon as any one dares to say anything about you, Matron heaps a beastly lot of mending on to them, so that they have to miss games and swimming. Anyway, Eileen, I warn you – you've got to tell your mother nice things about me, or I'll tell tales of *you*, and say I've seen Eddie and he didn't want his mother to know!"

Eileen bit her lip. It was very hard to keep her temper during this long speech. But she knew she had to, for Eddie's sake.

"I've apologized to you, Angela, and I've promised you what you want," she said, in a low voice. "Please give me the note now."

Angela fished in her pocket for the note. She was a

long time about it, pretending she had lost it, feeling in her blouse for it as well as in her pockets. Eileen hated her for this petty meanness, but she stood waiting patiently whilst Angela looked.

At last Angela produced the note. Eileen snatched it from her and without another word went off by herself to read it. It was very short.

DARLING SIS, (said the note)
I must see you. Don't say a word to Mother. We simply must have a talk. Can you meet me outside the garden-door in the wall, any time this evening? I'll wait behind a bush till you come.
            Your loving brother,
                        EDDIE.

Eileen read the note three times and then tore it up. She was afraid her mother might find it, and then she would be angry with Eddie. Mother wasn't very sympathetic, somehow. She didn't seem to think much of Eddie, and was always telling him what a fine man his father had been and how curious it was that Eddie hadn't done much good at school, or won any scholarships, or made her really proud of him.

"I'll slip down to the garden-door and see Eddie as soon as all the others are safely in the common room," thought Eileen, "Poor old Eddie – he must have been waiting a long time. He couldn't send a letter through the post, because Mother would have been sure to see it, and would have asked to read it."

The girl waited until she saw that all the fourth-formers were in their common room. She sat by the door and watched them. Doris and Carlotta were fooling about and the others were watching them, laughing. Claudine got up to join the two who were clowning, and Eileen saw that now was her chance. She slipped out.

But one person saw her go. That was Angela, who

had been expecting Eileen to slip away down to the lane. It was forbidden for the girls to go out of the school grounds without permission after evening prep, and Angela smiled spitefully to herself.

"If Eileen makes a habit of meeting dear brother Eddie out of hours, I shall be able to hold that over her, too," thought Angela. She went out of the room and walked into a little music-room that overlooked the school grounds. It was difficult to see any one in the trees and bushes, but because she knew exactly where to look, Angela was able to catch a glimpse of Eileen now and again, hurrying through the trees to the little gate in the wall.

She went back to the common room. Doris, Carlotta and Claudine were still fooling about, keeping every one in fits of laughter. Doris was a wonderful mimic, Carlotta could do extraordinary tricks, and Claudine could imitate Mam'zelle, her aunt, to perfection.

Angela could not see anything to laugh at at all. "Do they really think it's funny, to pull faces and make themselves ugly and stupid-looking?" she thought to herself, as she watched Doris imitating an old char-woman, and Claudine playing up to her as a French maid. She patted her beautiful pale gold hair, comparing it with Carlotta's wild mop. A smug little smile came on her lovely face. She knew she was more beautiful than any other girl in the school! What did brains and gifts matter? Every one stared at her in the street, every one thought she must be a princess at least. And perhaps one day she would marry a prince and be a real princess! Angela dreamed away, not listening to the chatter around her at all.

Two people watched her, one with envy and the other with devoted admiration. The first was Pauline, who, plain and unattractive, envied Angela her beauty, and longed with all her heart to look like her. But her own perfectly straight hair, well-brushed as it was, would never shine like Angela's, nor would it curl under at the ends, as Angela's did, so prettily. Angela's eyes were a brilliant, startling blue – Pauline's were pale. Angela's cheeks were a beautiful rosy pink. Pauline's seldom had any colour. It was too bad that Angela had so much and she, Pauline, had so little in the way of looks!

The other person watching Angela, was, of course, her devoted slave, Alison. She wondered if Angela had forgiven her for offering advice about Eileen. She tried to catch Angela's eye, but Angela was lost in beautiful day-dreams.

"You do look so lovely, Angela," whispered Alison, at last. Angela heard and smiled prettily. She had forgotten that she was offended with Alison. She spoke to her in a low voice, boasting of her conquest of Eileen.

"I ticked Eileen off properly for being a sneak," she said to Alison. "I forbade her ever to sneak again, and she promised she wouldn't."

"Oh, Angela – did you really make her promise that?" said Alison. "You're wonderful, you really are!" She looked round the common room. "I say – where *is* Eileen?"

"Would you like to know?" said Angela, looking at the expensive gold watch on her wrist, and seeing that there were only five minutes to go before bed-time. "Well, come with me and I'll see if I can show you where our dear Eileen is!"

She took Alison into the little music-room. "See the school wall, right down there?" she said. "You know the little door let into it there, behind the tennis-courts? Well, I think Eileen has gone through there into the lane to talk to dear, darling Eddie!"

"Look – is that Eileen coming back?" said Alison. "Golly, she'll get into a row if she's caught!"

"Yes – it's Eileen all right," said Angela, as a figure came into view between the trees and then disappeared again. "Let's wait outside the common-room door and catch her as she comes in!"

So the two waited there. Eileen came quickly up the passage to the room, and Angela spoke to her.

"Well – how's dear darling Eddie?"

Eileen stared at her, hardly seeming to see her. She looked pale and worried. She pushed at the shut door of the common-room, meaning to go and fetch her nightdress, which she had been mending. But Angela stopped her.

"You didn't answer my question," she said, in a smooth little voice. "How's dear darling Eddie?"

Eileen faced the spiteful girl. "Eddie's all right," she said, in a trembling voice. "Eddie's fine. He had lots of good news to tell me. He's getting on well."

She went into the common-room. Alison felt uncomfortable again. She didn't like this teasing, there was something spiteful in it – but how could she dare to find fault with the Honourable Angela?

Claudine gets her Own Way

"This is a jolly nice term," said Pat to Isabel, as they dried themselves after swimming in the big bathing-pool. "I simply adore all this open-air life – tennis and swimming and riding and gardening – and today we even had lessons out-of-doors, it was so hot!"

Isabel grinned. "Poor old Claudine doesn't like the open air as much as we do!" she said. "Wasn't she funny in maths?"

Claudine had indeed been funny. To begin with she had been quite horrified to hear that Miss Ellis proposed to take lessons out-of-doors under the trees. Apparently no school she had ever been to had ever thought of doing such a thing.

"Lessons out-of-door!" said the little French girl. "But why? What is the matter with indoors? I do not like this out-of-doors – the sun is too hot, it burns me."

"Pity it doesn't burn you a bit more," grinned Bobby, who was as brown as an acorn. "Look at us, all brown and tanned – and you are like a lily, pale and white."

Claudine looked down at her lily-white hands with great satisfaction. "That is another thing I do not understand about you so-jolly English girls," she said. "It is not pretty to get burnt, it is ugly to grow freckles – and yet you try to grow as brown as you can, all day long! Me, I like to be white-skinned. It is more natural, more becoming. And now – what can Miss Ellis be thinking of to say lessons out-of-doors! I shall take a sunshade with me, for I will not grow one single freckle."

But Miss Ellis did not approve of sunshades being brought out in a maths lesson. She looked at Claudine with disapproval. "I don't know if you are merely being funny, Claudine, or if you seriously think that you need a sunshade under the trees, where there is no sun – but whatever your reason, the sunshade must go back to the school at once. I can't imagine where you got it!"

The sunshade had been used in a play, and was simply enormous. Claudine was quite lost under it. She looked at Miss Ellis pathetically.

"Please, *chère* Miss Ellis, I am not making a joke, it is because I do not wish to grow a freckle on my nose," she said, beseechingly. "A freckle is not for a French girl. Freckles are English, Miss Ellis, and I do not want to grow them."

"Oh, freckles can be French as much as English!" said Miss Ellis. "It will do your pale face good to have a few nice brown freckles here and there, Claudine.

44

Take the sunshade back, please, and don't bring it out again."

"Oh please, Miss Ellis, couldn't Claudine and I share the sunshade?" said Angela, who also had a fear of freckles. Her face was tanned a rosy-brown, and she had no freckles at all – she was careful not to get too sun-burnt, for she knew that would spoil her delicate beauty. She gave Bobby's face a scornful glance. It was absolutely covered with little brown freckles, right to the tip of the up-turned nose. "I couldn't bear to get freckles like poor Bobby," went on Angela, no spite showing in her smooth little voice. "This sun is so hot, Miss Ellis – just see how it has treated Bobby!"

"Don't you believe it," said Bobby, not standing any nonsense of that sort. "My face is freckled winter and summer alike. Nothing to do with the summer sun! I was born with freckles!"

The class giggled, and Bobby opened her mouth to continue. But Miss Ellis knew Bobby's speeches, and spoke first!

"That will do, Bobby. I don't want any more of the maths lesson wasted on freckles. Claudine, take the sunshade back. Angela, don't look as if you are going to faint away – it would do both you and Claudine good to get a few freckles – Claudine because she sits too much indoors, and you because you think too much of your looks. It would be better if you thought a little more about your work. You may think it is amusing to be bottom each week, as you have been so far, but I must say I can't see the joke."

Angela flushed. How horrid Miss Ellis could be! She caught a satisfied smile on Pauline's face. Pauline was cleverer than Angela – that was one way in which she was better than Angela, anyhow! Angela scowled and glanced at Alison for comfort. Alison gave it, smiling adoringly, and making a face at Miss Ellis.

Lessons out-of-doors were not a success at all, with

45

Claudine in the class. She screamed whenever an insect flew near, and if a bird dared to fly suddenly out of a bush, she made every one jump by her yells. Miss Ellis got very tired of her.

"*Now* what's the matter, Claudine?" she said, when a bee flew near the girl and hummed in her ear. Claudine had squealed, jumped up and run to the other end of the long table on which everyone was working.

"It is an animal that goes 'Zzzz' and carries a sting, Miss Ellis," said Claudine, looking genuinely frightened.

"A bee," said Miss Ellis, in disgust. "It won't sting you. Sit down. You are disturbing all the others."

The next thing that upset Claudine was an ant. It crawled up her leg and she suddenly felt it. She gave such an agonized yell that every one jumped violently.

"CLAUDINE! I shall send you indoors if you squeal again!" said Miss Ellis in exasperation. "What's the matter now?"

Claudine was undoing her suspender with trembling hands, giving little squeals and French exclamations all the time. The ant had explored the inside of the top of her stocking. The girls went into fits of laughter, and Miss Ellis rapped angrily on her table.

"Claudine, what are you doing? Surely you are not taking off your stockings!"

Claudine was deaf to anything that Miss Ellis said. When she at last saw the ant, inside her stocking, she did not dare to touch it, and gazed round with such an agonized expression on her face that Bobby took pity on her, and flicked the ant deftly on to the grass.

"Ah!" said Claudine. "*Merci bien*, Bobbee! What a terrible thing to happen to me!"

"Much more terrible things will happen to you if I have any more disturbance," said Miss Ellis, in such a grim tone that Claudine was much astonished. She sat down again, doing up her suspender.

46

Everyone jumped as Claudine gave an agonized yell

"One more squeal from you and you go indoors," said Miss Ellis. Claudine gazed at her thoughtfully. If there was one thing more than another that Claudine wanted at that moment it was to go indoors, where creatures that flew and crawled did not molest her.

She waited until Miss Ellis had bent her head to correct Hilary's book, and then she let out a piercing yell that made her neighbour, Pauline, jump so violently that she upset the ink over the table. Miss Ellis leapt to her feet, her usual calmness quite deserting her.

"Claudine! This behaviour is intolerable. Go indoors at once and find the Mistress in the teachers' common room who is free at the moment. Tell her I sent you in in disgrace and ask her to let her sit with you, whilst you do your maths. And if there is a single mistake in your paper I shall have a great deal to say about it. I am thoroughly displeased with you."

With the greatest cheerfulness and alacrity Claudine obeyed Miss Ellis, scurrying indoors with her books before the mistress could change her mind. Doris exploded into one of her giggles. Miss Ellis glanced at her sharply, and Doris subsided. It then occurred to Miss Ellis that Claudine, as usual, had got exactly what she wanted, in her usual unscrupulous way!

Miss Ellis wondered who the mistress was who would be in the teachers' common room just then. She thought it would be Miss Rollins. That was good. Miss Rollins was very strict, and would make Claudine feel very small and humble before she had done with her.

But it was not Miss Rollins, much to Claudine's delight. When she knocked timidly on the mistress's common room door, she ran over in her mind what mistress was likely to be there. She hoped it would be the art mistress – she had a sense of fun and was very jolly.

She opened the door and went in – and she saw that it was Mam'zelle! Mam'zelle was having a cosy time by herself. She had taken off her big, flat-heeled shoes and had opened the collar of her high-necked blouse. It was such a hot day! She was half-asleep over her exercise books when the small neat figure of Claudine appeared. They stared at each other.

"Why are you here, Claudine?" asked Mam'zelle severely, in French. Claudine at once poured out a voluble and heart-rending explanation – how all the insects and winged beasts of that horrible English out-of-doors had molested her, yes, and bitten her and stung her, and altogether made life not worth living. And the sun had burnt her and she was sure she had dozens of those so-ugly freckles coming, and what would her dear mother say to that? Ah, life was very very hard at this so-sporting English school, with its love for the cold, cold water, and for striking at balls so many times a week, and for its detestable nature-walks, and . . .

Mam'zelle sympathized whole-heartedly. She too detested too much sun, and insects and reptiles of any kind filled her with fear and disgust. She forgot to inquire whether Claudine had come in of her own accord, or had been sent in in disgrace. Soon the two were talking nineteen to the dozen, going back in their thoughts to their beloved France, where girls were proper girls, and studied and did sewing and embroidery, and did not rush about in the mad way that all English girls did.

So, later on, when Miss Ellis asked Mam'zelle if she had scolded Claudine properly for being sent indoors in disgrace, Mam'zelle got a shock. She stared at Miss Ellis in dismay.

"Ah, the poor little Claudine!" she said at last. "You must not be too hard on her, Miss Ellis. It is so difficult for a poor little foreign girl to learn your English ways."

Miss Ellis snorted. "I suppose that means that you and Claudine patted each other on the back, and that you believed everything the naughty little girl said – and I should think it is very likely that you helped her

49

to do her maths too! She has never got all her sums right before."

Mam'zelle felt extremely uncomfortable. She *had* helped Claudine with her work – and certainly she had believed every word she said. Would Claudine deceive her own good aunt? No, no – impossible!

But when Mam'zelle thought things over she knew that the clever little Claudine could and would deceive her if she felt inclined to. Mam'zelle loved Claudine very much, and thought the world of her – but all the same sometimes a doubt came into her mind – wasn't Claudine just a little *too* clever? Didn't she get her own way just a little *too* often? The trouble was – you never knew what Claudine wanted until she had got it, and then it was too late to do anything about it.

"My word," said Bobby, when the maths lesson came to an end and the girls packed up their books. "That little monkey of a Claudine can do anything she likes and get away with it! I bet she's had a perfectly lovely time indoors."

So she had. She came beaming to meet Miss Ellis at the end of the morning, with a prettily-worded apology.

"Ah, Miss Ellis! I am so, so ashamed of myself. You English, you are not frightened of anything, you keep the hairs on your head always, always you are calm – but me, I am a silly little French girl, so please excuse me and I will do better in future. My aunt was very, very angry with me, she caused me to cry bitterly, see how red my eyes are!"

Miss Ellis saw no signs of red eyes, and felt quite certain that Mam'zelle had not been angry at all. All the same, she found it difficult to hide a smile. Claudine was so very, very earnest and apologetic!

"I'll forgive you *this* time, Claudine," she said. "But you be careful *next* time!"

Although the girls knew quite well that Claudine told fibs when it suited her, borrowed without asking and still copied answers from other people's books if she wanted to, they couldn't help liking her. She was very funny, generous in her own way, and never took offence whatever was said to her.

She might easily have taken offence at things that Angela said, or Pauline. Angela looked down on her in the same way that she looked down on Eileen – because she was a pupil who was probably not paying the school fees.

"Charity-girls, both of them!" she said to Alison, scornfully. "I must say I didn't think we'd get them at schools like this."

If Bobby, Hilary or the twins overheard things like this they ticked Angela off unmercifully.

"Look here," Pat said once, "we don't like Eileen any more than you do – but you've got to realize, Angela, that if Eileen's mother gets Eileen here for nothing, it's because of the work she does herself as Matron, and it doesn't matter tuppence if you pay for things in work or in money, it's good payment just the same, and Eileen isn't kept by 'charity' as you call it. You're a disgusting little snob."

Angela hated to be called a snob. She shut her book with a bang. "Snob!" she said. "That's a favourite word of yours for some one who happens to be out of the top drawer. Think of something more original to say."

51

"Right," said Bobby, at once. "You think that Claudine is a charity-girl too – well, instead of saying that to us, what about saying it to Mam'zelle – or even to Claudine herself? You're too cowardly to do that. You'll hit at Eileen because you've got some hold over her and she can't hit back – but you daren't hit at Claudine openly, because she's quite likely to fly at you and scratch your angelic face, or put Mam'zelle on the war-path after you!"

"Oh, you're impossible!" said Angela, angrily. "I shall ask my mother to take me away at half-term. In fact, when she comes here and sees what kind of girls I have to live with I'm certain she'll take me away with her, then and there!"

"Golly! If only your mother would be sensible enough to *do* that!" sighed Bobby. "But she won't. I know mothers. She'll leave you here to be a pest to us for the rest of the term."

Tears of anger came into Angela's eyes. In all her spoilt, petted life she had never been spoken to like this. She was angry, hurt, and miserable. She blinked back her tears, because a tear-stained face spoilt her beauty. She went to find Alison.

Alison could always put soothing ointment on to Angela's wounds. In her usual feather-headed way she made herself quite blind to Angela's grave faults, and saw only the loveliness of Angela's face, and the beauty of her clothes and possessions. Poor Alison always seemed to attach herself to the wrong kind of people.

"She'll never learn!" said Hilary. "I did think once, when she was in the second form, and was so keen on that awful drama mistress, Miss Quentin, that she had learnt a pretty sharp lesson – you remember how Miss Quentin let her down, don't you? She pretended to be awfully fond of Alison, and then laughed at her behind her back."

The twins nodded. "Yes," said Pat. "It's really a pity

that Alison isn't happy unless she is worshipping some-one. She's awfully bad for Angela. As soon as we get a bit of sense into Angela's head, Alison gets it out, by saying she's wonderful, too lovely for words, and all the rest of it."

"I must say she's not a bit like you two," said Bobby. "You've got plenty of common sense. It's funny you should have a cousin like Alison!"

The weather went on being hot and sunny, with blue skies every day. The girls swam and played games to their hearts' content. They all got very brown, except Claudine who managed to remain pale as a lily in spite of everything. She worried very much one week be-cause she felt sure she had a freckle coming on her nose. The girls teased her unmercifully.

"Golly! Isn't Claudine's freckle getting pro-nounced?" said Hilary, staring at Claudine's dainty little nose.

"Yes. It's going to be a real beauty," said Pat.

"Big as a threepenny bit," said Isabel.

Claudine gave a squeal of horror and fished out the little mirror she always carried with her. She and Angela and Alison always carried small mirrors about with them, and were for ever examining their faces for something or other.

"I have no freckle," she announced indignantly. "You talk under your hats!"

The girls laughed. "Claudine, you talk *through* your hat, not under it," said Bobby. "But if you want to keep a secret you keep it *under* your hat! See?"

Claudine sighed. "Ah, your English sayings are so difficult. I will remember – to talk *through* your hat means to be silly – to keep something *under* your hat means to keep a secret. Ah – there goes one who keeps something under her hat!"

The girls turned to see who Claudine meant. It was Eileen Paterson.

"Yes – Eileen does seem to be all bottled up, somehow," said Hilary, rather worried. "As if she's got a secret and is afraid some one will get to know it. She's been looking rather miserable sometimes."

"Well, she's got her mother here to tell anything to," said Pat. The others made scornful noises.

"Pooh!" said Bobby, "would *you* tell Matron anything if she were *your* mother? I know I wouldn't. She's as hard as nails! I hope to goodness I'm never ill whilst she's here as Matron. I shouldn't fancy being looked after by her!"

The girls were all rather careful in the way they treated Eileen now, because they felt certain that any slight, intended or otherwise, that they showed Eileen, was reported to Matron, and then Matron landed them with all kinds of unexpected mending to do. All except Angela. Angela could say and do what she liked to Eileen. Matron always seemed to look on Angela with a favourable eye. Eileen did not dare to tell tales of her.

"I think Eileen misses that dear brother of hers," said Bobby. "You know what Angela told us – how he came to see her, but didn't want to see his mother. I bet he's in some kind of trouble, and Eileen's worried about it."

"Poor Eileen!" said Hilary. "I'll just pump her a bit and see."

So Hilary kindly and tactfully 'pumped' Eileen, but she learnt very little.

"How old is your brother, Eileen?" she said. "Is he like you at all?"

Eileen fetched a snapshot and showed it to Hilary. She seemed glad of the chance of talking about Eddie.

"Eddie's eighteen," she said. "Two years older than I am. He's fine, Hilary. But he's never had much chance. You see, my father died when we were so little. Eddie ought to be at college now, but he's got to earn his living."

Hilary looked at the snap of the rather weak-looking

boy in the picture. He looked kind but that was about all one could say.

"What work is he doing?" she asked.

"He's in engineering works," she said. "He's doing awfully well. He'll make a lot of money one day."

"You're not worried about him, are you?" said Hilary, kindly, looking at the flushed face of the girl beside her.

Eileen answered at once. "Worried about him. Of course not! Why should I be? I wish I saw him more often, that's all. You see, until this term, when Mother took this job, we all lived together. Now he's in lodgings and I do miss him a lot."

Hilary said no more. She still thought that Eileen looked worried, and certainly she did not pay as much attention to her lessons as Miss Ellis expected – but after all, thought Hilary, it was enough to make any one look worried if they had to listen to Matron's grumbles in their spare-time!

Eileen had to help her mother with the school linen every week, and sometimes when the girls passed Matron's room they could hear her grumbling away at Eileen. True, Eileen answered back sometimes, but usually she listened in silence. Some of the girls felt sorry for Eileen, others were glad, because they knew she was a tale-teller when it suited her to pass on things she had heard in the fourth form.

Another week or two went by, and half-term began to come near. Three or four fourth-form birthdays came along too, and there was a good deal of present-buying.

Angela had unlimited pocket-money and bought most extravagant presents. Pauline tried to vie with her and to buy marvellous gifts too. But it was impossible to spend as much as Angela did! She thought nothing of spending ten shillings on a bottle of bath salts or a lace-edged handkerchief.

Eileen gave no presents at all. "Sorry," she said to

Hilary, whose birthday it was. "I'd like to give you something – but I've no money at the moment. Many happy returns of the day, anyway!"

"Thanks," said Hilary, thinking that Eileen could be very straightforward and honest, and liking her at that moment for being courageous enough to own up to having no money at all.

Angela presented Hilary with a magnificent blotter, made of real leather, and decorated very beautifully at the corners. Hilary liked it very much. Then Pauline presented her with a purse on which were Hilary's initials, H.W.W.

"Oh, Pauline – how beautiful!" said Hilary. "But I wish you wouldn't spend so much money on me! I'm sure you can't afford it!"

This was an unfortunate remark to make to Pauline, who was very touchy about money, and was always trying to compete with Angela. She flushed and answered stiffly.

"You know that my family, the Bingham-Joneses, are wealthy," she said, putting on the affected voice that Hilary detested. "I have as much money as I wish. It's true I don't splash it about in the vulgar way that Angela does – I hope I am better-bred than that. But I have all I ask for, Hilary, so please accept this purse with my best wishes, and don't think it cost any more than I could afford!"

"What with the Bingham-Joneses and the Honourable Favorleighs we're just overwhelmed with high-and-mightiness!" said Pat to Isabel, with a giggle. "Well – I think I prefer Pauline of the two – Angela is really too spiteful for words, sometimes – and she says the cattiest things with the most angelic smile on her face!"

"I can't say I think a great deal of any of the four new girls, considering everything," said Isabel, wrinkling her forehead and thinking. "Angela's a spiteful snob. Pauline is an envious snob. Claudine is

56

amusing but quite unscrupulous – hasn't any sense of honour at all, as far as I can see – and Eileen is a sneak and a bit of a bore!"

"Golly – you sound pretty catty yourself, Isabel!" said Pat.

"No, I'm not," said Isabel, earnestly. "I'm only just sizing them all up. I'm not like Alison, unable to see beyond a pretty face. And though I don't think much of any of those four, you know jolly well I'd help every one of them if they were in trouble. And if you're really catty, you don't feel like that, do you?"

"No, you don't," said Pat. "You're quite right, old thing – it doesn't matter seeing people for what they are, and even disliking them – so long as you're willing to help if necessary!"

Preparing for Half-term

Half-term came along very shortly, and the girls were excited because their parents were coming to see them. There were to be tennis-matches and swimming-matches for the parents to watch. Hilary, Bobby, the twins and one or two others were excited about these, because they hoped to be in the teams.

"I'd like my mother to see me swim under water for the whole length of the bath," said Bobby. "She was a very good swimmer herself when she was young. Hope I'm chosen for the swimming-competitions."

The twins hoped to be in one of the tennis-matches. They were both good at tennis, and it would be lovely for their mother to see them play together and win a match. Both girls were intensely proud of St. Clare's, and badly wanted to show off their school, and their own prowess to the best advantage.

Hilary was to play in a singles match with one of the fifth-formers. She had been chosen for her very graceful style, and it was to be an exhibition match more than a battle. Both girls had a beautiful natural style and the games-mistress was proud of them.

Mirabel was hoping to win the one-length race in the swimming-bath. She was very fast and very strong. Her small friend, the mouse-like Gladys, was also in the swimming competitions, for, although she was small, she was a beautiful little swimmer. She was longing for her mother to see her. She had no father and no brother or sister, so her mother was everything to her.

"Half-term will be fun," said Hilary. "Is your mother coming, Angela?"

"Of course," said Angela. "And Daddy too. I'm longing to see their new car. It's a Rolls-Bentley, black with a green line, and . . ."

"I bet you're looking forward to seeing the new car more than to seeing your people!" said Bobby, with a chuckle. "You never talk of your parents except in terms of the wealth they own, Angela. Did you know that?"

Angela looked sulky. "I don't know what you mean," she said. "I guess you'd talk about cars and things if your parents had the same as mine. And you just see my mother when she comes! She will stand out above every one else. She's absolutely beautiful – golden hair like mine – and the bluest eyes – and she wears the most marvellous clothes . . ."

"And even the safety-pins she uses are made of pure gold set with diamonds," finished Pat.

"That's not funny," said Angela, as the others shouted with laughter. "I tell you, you just wait and see my mother! She's the most beautiful person you'll ever see."

"*What* a pity you don't take after her, Angela!" said Bobby, sorrowfully. "Isn't your mother sorry to have a daughter like you? You must be a terrible disappointment."

Angela flushed with anger. She could never bear this kind of teasing. "All right," she said, in a bitter voice. "All right. But just wait till you see my mother – and then tell me if she isn't the most wonderful person you ever saw in your lives. I hope she wears her doublestring of pearls. They are worth five thousand pounds."

"Well," said the soft voice of Gladys, who rarely butted in on any conversation of this sort, "well, I don't care if *my* mother wears her very oldest clothes, I don't care if she's got a ladder in her stockings, I don't care if she's hasn't even powdered her nose – so long as my mother comes to see me and I can be with her for a few hours, she can be the untidiest, ugliest, poorest-dressed there – but I shall still be proud of her, and think she's the best of all!"

This was a long speech for the timid Gladys to make. Ever one was silent when she stopped. Pat found that she suddenly had tears in her eyes. There was such love in Gladys's voice – and what she said was fine. That was the way to love some one – not to care how they looked or what they did – but just to welcome them all the same!

Even Angela was taken aback. She stared at Gladys in surprise. She was about to make a sneering remark but Bobby stopped her.

"Now you shut up," said Bobby, in a warning voice. "Gladys has said the last words about mothers, and she's right. Good for you, Gladys."

After that Angela said no more, but privately she rejoiced when she thought of her own beautifully-dressed mother, and how the girls would have to admire her and her clothes when she came.

"Are *your* parents coming?" said Hilary to Pauline.

"Oh yes," said Pauline, in a bright voice, and she began to talk eagerly of them. "My Father is such a good-looking man, and Mother is sweet. I do hope she wears the dress she bought in the holidays – it's really beautiful. It makes her look so young and pretty."

Pauline chattered away about her parents, in her way as much of a snob as Angela, though, far more than Angela, she talked of them as real people, generous, kind, amusing, instead of people cluttered up with great possessions.

"Pauline's people sound rather nice," said Pat. "I shall take a good look at Angela's family – I sort of feel that her father will wear diamond buttons on his coat and her mother will wear five or six furs at once!"

Isabel giggled. "Well, I'm rather glad that our mother is just ordinary," she said, "pretty and kind and sensible, just an ordinary nice mother!"

The girls all practised hard for half-term, swimming and playing tennis was much as they could, so that their parents might be proud of them. There was to be an exhibition of pictures too, done by the girls themselves, and a show of needlework. Here Claudine expected to shine. She had done a really beautiful cushion-cover, on which was embroidered a peacock spreading its lovely tail.

Mam'zelle was intensely proud of this. She bored every one by talking about it. "It is exquisite!" she said. "Ah, the clever little Claudine! Miss Ellis, do you not think that Claudine has done the tail most perfectly?"

"I do," said Miss Ellis. "Much better than she does her maths or her history, or her geography or her literature, or her . . ."

"Come, come!" said Mam'zelle, hurt. "It is not given

60

to us to have great gifts at everything. Now, the little Claudine, she . . ."

"I don't expect Claudine to have great gifts at anything but needlework," said Miss Ellis. "All I ask is a *little* attention in class, and a *little* thought in prep time! You spoil Claudine, Mam'zelle."

"I! I spoil Claudine!" cried Mam'zelle, her glasses falling off her nose in rage. "I have never spoilt any girl, never. Always I am strict, always I am fair, always I am . . ."

"All right, Mam'zelle," said Miss Ellis, hastily, seeing that Mam'zelle was going to make one of her long and impassioned speeches, "all right. I must go. You can tell it all to me when you see me next."

Mam'zelle sought out Claudine. She fell upon her and hugged her, much to Claudine's surprise. But it had suddenly occurred to Mam'zelle that "the poor little Claudine" would not have parents visiting her at half-term, for they were in France. So, immediately on thinking this, she had gone to comfort Claudine, who, however, was not in any need of comfort at all. She liked her parents, but as she was one of a very large family, and had only got a small share of their love and attention, she had not missed them very much.

"Ah, my little Claudine!" said Mam'zelle, flinging her arms round the astonished Claudine. "Do not be sad, do not be discouraged! Do not fret yourself – you shall not be alone at half-term."

Claudine wondered if her aunt had gone mad. "I am not sad, *ma tante*," she said. "What is the matter? Has anything happened?"

"No, no," said Mam'zelle, still full of tender thoughts for her little Claudine, "nothing has happened. It is only that I feel for you because your parents will not be with you at half-term. When every one else has their handsome fathers and their so-beautiful mothers, you will have no one – no one but your loving Aunt Mathilde!"

"Well, that's okay," said Claudine in English. Mam'-zelle wrinkled up her nose and her glasses fell off.

"Do not use these expressions!" she said. "They are vulgar. Ah, my little Claudine, you will not have any parents to admire your so-fine cushion-case with its magnificent peacock – but I will be there, my little one, I will stand by your cushion-cover all the time, not one minute will I go away, and I will say to every one: 'See! See the beautiful cover made by the clever Claudine! Ah, it needs a French girl to do such work as this! Regard the tail, regard each feather so finely-done in silk, regard the priceless cushion-cover, the most beautiful thing in this school today'!"

"Oh, Aunt Mathilde, I wish you wouldn't think of saying anything like that," said Claudine in alarm. "The girls would laugh like anything. They would tease me terribly. Please don't. I shan't be lonely. I shan't mind not having any one there."

"Ah, the brave little one!" sighed Mam'zelle, wiping away a tear from her eye. "I see your courage. You will not show others that you suffer."

"I *shan't* suffer," said Claudine, getting impatient. "I shan't really, Aunt Mathilde. Please don't make a fuss like this. It would be dreadful if you stood by my cushion-cover all the afternoon and made remarks like that."

The idea of Mam'zelle standing like a bull-dog on guard, telling surprised parents of her poor lonely little Claudine, and praising to the skies the little cushion-cover filled Claudine with horror. She began to wish that half-term was safely over.

But it hadn't even come. Four days away – three days – two days – the night before. Ah, now it really *was* near! The girls went to bed very excited that night and talked in whispers long after lights were out. Susan

Howes, the head-girl of the form, pretended to be asleep. She could not bear to be a spoil-sport on the night before half-term, strict as she was on all other nights.

Angela was thinking of the wonderful impression her mother would make, and how she would bask in her reflected glory. She hoped her mother would wear her famous pearls – and that wonderful fox fur.

Eileen was thinking about her own mother. She would be there as Matron, not all dressed up and pretty as other people's mothers would be. She wished that Eddie could be there – not because she was going to do anything in the swimming or tennis matches, or had anything in the art or needle work exhibition – but because it would have been lovely to have seen him looking for her – her own darling big brother!

Alison was looking forward to seeing her own pretty mother, and also to seeing Angela's mother too. She hoped the two would be friends. It would be lovely if they liked one another, and what fun if Angela's mother asked her, Alison, to stay with them in the holidays. That *would* be fine!

Pauline was thinking of her parents too. So was Bobby. It seemed a long time since the last holidays. School was fun – but your own home and people were something very solid and real and lovely. It would be nice to get a bit of them tomorrow.

One by one the girls fell asleep. Bobby was the first to wake up. She sat up and spoke loudly. "Wake up, you sleepy-heads! It's half-term!"

Half-term at Last!

Half-term Saturday was a perfectly beautiful day. The sun shone down from a blue sky that hadn't a single cloud in it.

"Gorgeous, isn't it, Claudine?" said Doris happily to the little French girl. "Couldn't be better."

Claudine groaned. "To think we shall all have to be out-of-doors in this terrible sun!" she said. "I know I shall get a freckle. I wish it had rained."

"You spoil-sport!" said Bobby, grinning. "You would like to huddle indoors even on a day like this. Come on, cheer up and smile – it's really a heavenly day."

The art exhibition was all ready for the parents to admire. There were some really good pictures there. Miss Walker, the art mistress, was proud of them. She had a water-colour class which went out regularly to paint country scenes with her, and some of them were very good.

"Good enough to sell!" said Claudine. "Do we sell our work? How much would you get for this so-beautiful picture, Hilary?"

Hilary laughed. "You have got funny ideas, Claudine," she said. "Of course we don't sell our work. As if our proud parents would let us! No, they will take our pictures home, and our pottery, and place them in conspicuous places on the walls, or mantel-piece, so that all their friends can admire them, and say, 'How clever your daughter must be, Mrs. So-and-So!'"

"I bet your mother will be pleased if you send her that lovely cushion-cover of yours for her birthday," said Pat. Claudine laughed.

"I have three sisters who do much more beautiful work than I do," she said. "My mother would look at my cover and say, 'Ah! The little Claudine is improving! This is not bad for a beginning.'"

"Mam'zelle thinks it's wonderful, anyhow," said Bobby, grinning. "There's one thing about you, Claudine – you're not in the least conceited. With all the fuss that every one has made of your embroidery, you might quite well have begun to swank about it. But you don't."

"Ah, I know that it is good compared with the sewing of you English girls," said Claudine, seriously, "but, you see, I know that it would be quite ordinary in France. I have a different standard to compare that so-beautiful cover with, and I cannot think it is as wonderful as you do."

Claudine was a very funny mixture of honesty, sincerity and deceitfulness. Even her deceitfulness was queer, because she did not attempt to hide it. She often tried to deceive Miss Ellis, for instance, and if Miss Ellis saw through it, Claudine would at once admit to her attempted deceit without any shame. It was almost as if she were playing a game with the teachers, trying to get the better of them, but not trying to hide the fact that she *was* trying to get the better of them. The girls could not quite make her out.

Pat and Isabel were playing together in a school-match, and they were delighted. They looked out their white skirts and blouses, their red socks and white shoes, and took the clothes to Matron for the school-maid to iron. Every one had to look their best when parents came!

Pauline looked a little miserable at breakfast-time,

and the girls wondered why. Hilary spoke to her in her usual kindly way.

"What's up, Pauline? You're looking glum. You're not upset because you haven't been chosen to play in the school-matches, are you?"

"Oh no," said Pauline. "I've had a great disappointment, that's all."

"What?" asked Hilary, and the other girls came round to hear.

"Well, you see," said Pauline, "it's most unfortunate – Mother is ill, and my Father doesn't like to leave her – so they won't be coming today! And I was *so* looking forward to them being here and seeing everything."

"Bad luck, Pauline!" said the twins, sympathetically. A disappointment of that kind was awful at the last minute. Every one was very sorry.

"I hope your Mother isn't really ill," said Susan Howes.

"No, not seriously," said Pauline. "But she can't possibly come. Oh dear – and I did so badly want you all to see my good-looking Father and my pretty Mother. I even wrote to ask her if she would wear the pretty new frock I liked so much, and she said she would."

"Well, never mind," said Isabel, feeling very sorry indeed. "You can come out with us and our people, if you like, Pauline. Then you won't feel so lonely."

"Oh, thank you," said Pauline, and after that she seemed to cheer up a good deal, and entered into everything with enthusiasm.

Mam'zelle had displayed Claudine's beautiful cushion-cover in a very prominent place. She still seemed inclined to fall on Claudine's neck, and tell her she must not feel lonely, and the little French girl kept out of her way as much as possible, slipping deftly round the corner whenever she saw her aunt approaching.

"Sort of hide-and-seek you're playing, Claudine!" said Bobby. "You'll have to have a word with Mam'zelle soon, or she'll burst. She's longing to show you how beautifully she has arranged your so-marvellous cushion-cover!"

Lunch was a very scrappy affair that day because the maids were concerned with the strawberry tea that the parents were to have in the afternoon, and scores of pounds of strawberries were being prepared in big glass dishes. The cooks had made the most lovely cakes and biscuits, and there were sandwiches of every kind. The girls kept peeping into the big dining-room, where the dishes were all set out.

Claudine slipped in and sampled some of the strawberries. She was the only one who dared to do this.

"You'll get into a row if any one catches you," said Bobby.

"You go and taste them," said Claudine, running her pink tongue round her crimson lips. "They are so sweet and juicy!"

"No," said Bobby. "We've been put on our honour not to sample this afternoon's tea, and I wouldn't dream of breaking my honour."

"This honour of yours, it is a funny thing," said Claudine. "It is a most uncomfortable thing. It stops you from doing what you want to do. I have no honour to worry me. I will never have this honour of yours. I do not like it."

"You're awful, Claudine," said Angela, screwing up her nose. "You do exactly as you like. I'm glad I'm not as dishonourable as you are."

The tone was very unpleasant, but Claudine only laughed. She hardly ever took offence. "Ah, Angela!" she said, "you think it is worse to take a few strawberries than to tell untruths about another girl behind her back? Me, I think it is really dishonourable to speak lies against another girl as you do. To me you are dishonourable, a worth-nothing girl, not because of a few strawberries but because of your evil tongue!"

The listening girls laughed at this. It was said in a pleasant voice, but there was such such truth in it, and the tables had been turned so cleverly on Angela that the girls couldn't help being amused. Only Angela was angry. But there was little time to quarrel on half-term day. There were so many jobs to do, and every one had her own allotted task.

Some had to do the flowers all over the school, and this took a long time. The vases had to be washed, old flowers thrown away, new ones picked, and then arranged to the best advantage in all kinds of bowls, jars and vases. The twins were especially good at this, and were very busy all the morning.

After lunch every one changed into either sports frocks or school uniform. The summer uniform was a brightly-coloured tunic. The girls could choose any colour they liked, so every girl was able to wear the one that suited her best. Dark girls, like Carlotta, chose reds and oranges, fair girls like Angela chose pale colours, blues and pinks. They looked like flowers, moving about against the green lawns of the school grounds, on that hot summer day.

"The parents are arriving!" squealed Alison, as she heard the sound of wheels coming up the drive. "The first lot are here. Who are they?"

The fourth-formers looked out of their windows, but nobody knew the people in the car. "They must belong to some of the lower school," said Bobby. "Here come some more!"

"They're mine!" cried Janet. "Oh goody-goody! I hoped they'd come early. I say, doesn't my mother look nice and brown. I'm going to greet them."

She sped off happily. More and more cars drove up the drive, and soon the lawns were crowded with fathers and mothers and aunts, and with younger or older brothers and sisters. How Eileen wished that Eddie could be there!

Eileen's mother was very trim and starched in her Matron's uniform and white apron. Some of the parents went to talk to her about the health of their children. Eileen was glad that her mother was sought out by so many parents – but she could not help wishing that she had on a pretty frock and looked as sweet and attractive as many of the other girls' mothers.

"Mother ought to smile more," thought Eileen. "She looks so strict and hard. Look at the twins' mother over there – she's really sweet. And I do like the way she's got her arm round both Pat and Isabel. Mother never puts her arm round me or Eddie."

An enormours car rolled up the drive, with a smartly-uniformed chauffeur in front. It was a beautiful new Rolls-Bentley, black with a small green line. It came to a stop and the chauffeur got out. Angela gave a loud squeal.

"That's our new car! Look, every one, isn't it a beauty! And do you like the chauffeur's uniform, black with green piping to match the car? The cushions are black too, with green edges and green monograms."

"I should have thought you would have been so excited to see your parents that you wouldn't even have noticed the car!" said Janet's cool voice. But Angela took no notice. She was very pleased indeed that so many of the fourth-formers were near when her grand new car drove up!

The chauffeur opened the car-door. Angela's mother stepped out. Certainly she was a vision of beauty! She looked very young, was extraordinarily like Angela, and she was dressed in a most exquisite fashion.

The girls stared at her. She looked round with brilliant blue eyes, also very like Angela's. After her came her husband, a tall, soldierly-looking man, with rather a serious face. Angela gave another squeal.

She ran to her parents and flung her arms round her mother as she had seen the others do, purposely exaggerating everything because she knew they were watching.

"Angela dear! Be careful of my dress!" said her mother. "Let me see how you are looking."

Her father gave Angela a good hug, and then pushed her a little way away so that he could have a good look at her.

"She looks very well indeed," said her father.

"But this awful school uniform spoils her," said her mother. "I do think it is most unbecoming. And I can't bear those terrible school shoes, with their flat heels."

"Well, all the girls wear the same," said Angela's father, reasonably. "I think Angela looks very nice."

"If only the school had a prettier uniform!" said Angela's mother, in a complaining voice. "That was one reason why I didn't want to send her here – the dress was *so* ugly!"

Angela's 'Wonderful' Mother

The complaining voice of Angela's mother could be heard very often indeed that afternoon. Beautiful as she was, attractive and exquisite in her dress and looks, the lovely face was spoilt by an expression of discontent and boredom.

She complained of so many things, and her voice was unfortunately harsh and too loud! She complained of the hard bench that she had to sit on to watch the tennis-matches. She found fault with the cup of tea that Angela brought her. "What terrible tea They might at least provide China tea. You know I can't drink Indian tea, Angela."

She complained of the cake she took. "Awfully dry," she said. "I can hardly eat it."

"Leave it then," said Angela's father. And to Angela's horror her mother dropped the cake on the ground, where it could be trodden underfoot. The sharp eyes of the other girls noted all these things, and Angela began to feel rather uncomfortable.

"Isn't my mother lovely?" she whispered to Alison. "Don't you think those pearls are marvellous? Hasn't she got beautiful hair?"

Alison agreed. Privately she thought that Angela's mother acted like a spoilt child, complaining and grumbling all the time. She did not praise the pictures in the art exhibition, neither did she show any enthusiasm for the pottery work. She was forced to express a good opinion on Claudine's cushion-cover, because Mam'zelle stood there like a dragon, looking so fierce that every one felt they must praise her niece's handiwork.

"Ah! So this is your mother, Angela?" said Mam'zelle, in a most amiable voice. "We will show her the work of the little Claudine! Is it not beautiful? See the exquisite stitches! Regard the fine tail, spreading so well over the cover!"

Angela's mother looked as if she was going to pass the cover by without saying anything, but Mam'zelle was certainly not going to let that happen. She took hold of the visitor's arm and almost forced her to bend over Claudine's cushion-cover. "You have not seen it! It is a work of art! It is the finest thing in the exhibition!" said Mam'zelle, getting excited.

"Very nice," said Angela's mother, in a tone that seemed to say "Very nasty!" She took her arm away from Mam'zelle's hand, brushed her sleeve as if it had some dust left on it, and turned away impatiently.

"Who is that awful old woman?" she asked Angela,

71

in much too loud a voice. "Surely *she* doesn't teach you, my dear? Did you ever see any one look so dowdy?"

The girls were very fond of Mam'zelle, and they were angry to hear this remark. Bobby felt certain that Mam'zelle herself had caught some of it. The Frenchwoman was standing looking after Angela and her parents with a puzzled and hurt expression in her eyes.

"Well – I always thought Angela was pretty beastly," said Bobby to Pat, in a low tone, "and now I see where she gets her cattiness from! How ashamed I'd be of *my* mother if she walked round like that, criticizing things and people at the top of her voice. Poor old Mam'zelle! It's a shame to hurt her."

Claudine had overheard the remarks made by Angela's mother, and she too was hurt and angry. She was fond of her Aunt Mathilde, and thought she was cross with her for standing by her cushion-cover and behaving in such an exaggerated way about it, she saw that it was the intense love and pride she had for Claudine herself that made her do it.

She looked at Angela's beautiful mother. She noted her discontented face, and the petulant droop of the mouth that at times quite spoilt its loveliness. She thought of all the hurts and insults that that beautiful mouth must have uttered through the years. And Claudine longed to punish Angela's mother in some dramatic way for the cruel words she had spoken about her Aunt Mathilde!

Angela took her parents to the swimming-pool, St. Clare's was proud of this, for it was one of the finest and biggest swimming-pools owned by any school in the kingdom. The water lapped against the sides, a beautiful blue-green colour.

But even here Angela's mother had fault to find. "I suppose they change the water every day, Angela?" she said.

"No, Mother, twice a week, sometimes three times,"

said Angela. Her mother gave a little disgusted squeal.

"Good gracious! To think they can't even change the water every day! What a school! I really must make a complaint about it. Angela, you are not to bathe in the pool unless the water has just been changed I forbid it."

"But Mother," began Angela, uncomfortably. "I have to do what the others do – and really, the water *is* quite clean, even when it's two days old, or three."

"I shall complain," said Angela's mother. "I never did like the idea of sending you here. It's a second-rate school, I think. I wanted to send you to High Towers School. *Such* a nice school! I can't think why your father wanted to send you here. Perhaps now he has seen it he will think again."

"Pamela, don't talk so loudly," said Angela's father. "People here don't like to listen to what you are saying. You are in a minority – it is plain that all the other parents here think as *I* do – that St. Clare's is splendid in every way!"

"Oh, *you*," said Angela's mother, as if what her husband thought was of simply no account at all. She shut up her scarlet lips, and looked just as sulky as Angela always did when anybody ticked her off.

No – Angela's mother was certainly not a success! Beautiful she might be, expensive she certainly was – but she had none of the graciousness of the twins' mother, or the common sense of Bobby's jolly-looking mother, or the affection of Gladys's plainly-dressed but sweet-faced mother.

"I'm jolly glad I haven't got a mother like Angela's!" said Janet to Alison. "Isn't she perfectly awful?"

Loyal though Alison wanted to be to Angela, she couldn't help nodding her head. She had overheard many of Angela's mother's rude remarks, and she had not liked them, because even feather-headed Alison felt a deep sense of loyalty to St. Clare's and all it stood

73

for. She was not at all eager to be introduced to Angela's mother now – but the time came when she had to be, for Angela sought her out and took her off.

"Mother, this is Alison, the friend I told you about in my letters," said Angela. Her mother looked at the pretty, dainty girl with approval. Alison was like Angela, and could wear the school uniform well.

"Oh, so this is Alison," said Angela's mother, "How do you do? I must say you look a little more attractive than some of the girls here. One or two that Angela has introduced me to have been perfect frights!"

Bobby had been introduced to Angela's mother and was presumably one of the 'frights'. Her frank freckled face was not at all attractive to any one as exquisite as Angela's mother.

"Where is your mother?" asked Angela. "We must introduce her to mine. Mother wants to ask if you can spend some of the summer hols. with me."

But, rather to Alison's relief, when the introduction had been made, and the two mothers had greeted one another, the invitation was quite firmly declined by Alison's own mother!

"Thank you," she said. "but I am afraid I have other plans for Alison."

She did not explain what these were. She did not say that she had watched Angela's mother, and had heard some of her insolent remarks and detested them. She did not say that Angela's mother was the sort of person she would hate Alison to spend even a day with! But Alison knew what her mother was thinking, and silly girl as she was, she knew that her mother was right.

Angela's mother sensed that the other mother was snubbing her, and she was surprised and annoyed. She was about to say something more, when a bell rang loudly.

"Oh! Must they ring bells like that!" said Angela's mother, putting her hands to her ears. "How crude!"

"But sensible, don't you think so?" said Alison's mother drily, and left her.

"That's the bell to tell us to go and watch the swimming," said Alison, slipping her hand into her mother's arm. "Come on, Mummy. You'll see Bobby swimming there – you know, the freckled girl you liked. And Mirable too – she's awfully fast."

The hot sun blazed down as the company took its place round the swimming-pool. The parents sat at the edge of the baths, but the girls were in the big gallery above, watching eagerly.

Many of them were not taking part in the swimming, but they were all keen to see the performers diving, somersaulting and swimming. It was fun to hear the continual splashes, and to see the rippling of the blue water.

"Isn't it a gorgeous afternoon," said Janet, happily. "I *am* enjoying myself! I feel so glad that it's a fine day so that we can show off St. Clare's at its very best."

"All our parents seem to think it's a great success " said Bobby. "Well – except *one* parent!"

She meant Angela's mother. Angela heard this remark and flushed. She had been so pleased to show off her beautiful mother – but somehow everything had been spoilt now. She couldn't help wishing that her mother had made nice remarks like the others had made. But then, Mother wasn't usually very pleased with things, no matter what they were.

Claudine, Alison, Angela and many others not in the swimming, got front places in the big gallery above the water. Claudine leaned over rather far, not so much to look at the swimmers, in their navy-blue swim-suits, but to see the rows of parents.

"Look out, Claudine, you'll fall in!" said Alison, in alarm, trying to pull her back.

"I shall not fall," said Claudine. "I am just looking at the so-discontented person below, with the voice that makes loud and rude remarks!"

"Sh," said Alison. "Angela will hear you."

"I do not care," said Claudine. "Why should Angela expect us to praise a mother who is beautiful only in appearance, and whose character is ugly?"

"Do be quiet," said Alison, afraid that Angela would hear. "I'm sorry Angela's mother said that about your aunt, Claudine. I heard it, and I'm sure poor Mam'-zelle was hurt."

The swimming began. Angela's mother looked disgusted when a drop of water splashed on to her beautiful frock. She shook it daintily and tried to move backwards a little – but other people were behind her and she couldn't.

It was an exciting hour, for the swimmers were fast and good, and the divers graceful and plucky. But the most exciting bit of the whole afternoon was not the swimming or the diving, or the backward somersaulting done so cleverly by Bobby.

It was an unexpected and highly dramatic performance, quite unrehearsed, given by Claudine!

She was leaning well over the gallery balcony. She suddenly gave a piercing shriek that made every one jump in alarm – and then to the horror of all the lookers-on, the little French girl fell headlong from the gallery into the water below!

A Happy Time

She made a most terrific splash. The water rose up and fell all over Angela's mother, soaking her from head to foot!

"Good gracious!" said Miss Theobald, the Head Mistress, startled out of her usual calm dignity. "Who has fallen into the water? Get her out, quickly!"

Claudine could not swim. She sank under the water, and then rose to the surface, gasping. Bobby and Mirabel who were in the water, too, at once swam over to her. They got hold of her and helped her to the steps.

"Claudine! Whatever happened?" said Bobby. "You *are* an idiot!"

Claudine was gasping and spluttering. She cast an eye towards Angela's mother, and saw, to her delight, that she was drenched. Miss Theobald was by her, apologizing, and saying that she must come at once to the school, and allow her, Miss Theobald, to lend her some clothes whilst hers were drying.

Angrily Angela's mother followed the Head Mistress from the swimming-pool. She looked a dreadful sight, with her dress soaked and clinging tightly to her, and her beautiful hat dripping with water. Angela looked very distressed.

"You too, Claudine, you must go with Matron and get into dry clothes," said Miss Ellis to the soaking wet fourth-former. "Get into another tunic, quickly, or you'll catch cold. Hurry, now."

Claudine, out of the tail of her eye, saw Mam'zelle

77

Claudine cast an eye towards Angela's mother

bearing down upon her, alarm and anxiety written all over her. The little French girl at once fled off up to the school. She felt she could not bear to be enwrapped in Mam'zelle's overwhelming affection just then.

"Wait, wait, Claudine," called Matron, who was annoyed that Claudine had caused her to leave the company and go back to the school. But Claudine did not wait. Better to face Matron's annoyance rather than Mam'zelle's loud exclamations of dismay and sympathy!

"How exactly like Claudine to cause such a disturbance!" said Pat to Isabel. "Oh Isabel – I can't help feeling delighted that the person who got soaked was Angela's tiresome mother!"

"I suppose Claudine couldn't possibly have done it on purpose, could she?" said Isabel, doubtfully. "You know, she doesn't care in the least what she does, if she wants to get a result she has set her heart on. I bet she wanted to punish Angela's mother for her rudeness to Mam'zelle!"

"But Claudine simply hates and detests the water!" said Pat. "Nothing will make her undress and have a swim. And to let herself fall from the gallery into the water would be a very brave thing to do, considering she can't swim."

Claudine soon returned, in dry clothes, looking demure and innocent. She could look just as innocent as Angela when she liked – and now that the girls knew her better, they were certain that the more innocent Claudine looked, the worse mischief she had done or was about to do!

Angela's mother also returned, after a while – dressed in Miss Theobald's clothes! Miss Theobald was about the same size as Angela's mother, but a little taller, and although she always looked nice, her clothes were very simple, plain and dignified.

They did not suit Angela's mother at all. In fact she

79

looked very extraordinary in them and she knew it. She was angry and she showed it. It was bad enough to be drenched like that by some silly, careless girl, but much worse to be made to wear clothes too long for her, and so dowdy and frumpish after her own!

But somehow Angela's mother could not be rude to Miss Theobald. The Head Mistress was extremely kind and apologetic, but she was also calm and dignified, and she acted as if she expected Angela's mother to be calm and dignified also. And, much to her surprise, the spoilt woman found herself guarding her tongue and behaving quite well, whilst she changed into Miss Theobald's clothes.

The rest of the time went quickly. The matches and competitions were all over. Parents went off with their children, taking them out to dinner in the various hotels round about, for a treat.

Pauline went with Mrs. O'Sullivan, the twins' mother. The twins had told their mother about the girl's great disappointment, and she had at once said that Pauline must come with them.

Alison's mother spoke to Alison. "Is there any one you would like to bring with you this evening? I hope you don't want to go with Angela and her people, because your father and I would rather be on our own with you."

Alison understood that her mother had no wish to become at all friendly with Angela's mother. If she could choose some one to go with her, it would be easy to refuse Angela, if she asked for the two families to have dinner together. Alison wondered whom she could ask.

She took a look round at the girls. Most of them were clustered around their parents, chattering gaily, waiting for the various cars to come along. Eileen stood alone, watching. Her mother had disappeared – gone to see to some of the younger children, probably. The girl had such a forlorn look on her face that Alison was touched.

"I'll ask Eileen, Mother," she said. "I don't like her much – or her mother, who is Matron – but she would so enjoy coming! And oh, Mother – could I ask some one else too?"

"Who?" said her mother, in surprise.

"Could I ask Claudine, the little French girl who fell into the water?" said Alison. "Her parents are in France. She's only got her aunt here, Mam'zelle. I know she would simply love to come! She adores going out."

"All right, dear. Ask them both," said her mother, pleased. Anything rather than having that spoilt little Angela and her equally spoilt mother with them!

Alison tore off to Eileen. "Eileen. Go and ask your mother if you can come out to dinner with my people. Hurry up."

"Oh!" said Eileen, her eyes suddenly shining like stars. "Oh, Alison – do you really mean it? You *are* decent!"

She rushed off to find her mother. Alison went up to Claudine. "Claudine, will you come out with me and my people? Mother said I could ask you. Eileen is coming too."

"Thank you," said Claudine, all her pretty manners coming into play. "It is indeed very kind of you, Alison, and of your mother too. I will go to ask my aunt."

Mam'zelle was delighted. She liked Alison, although she despaired over her French. "Yes, you go, my little Claudine," she beamed. "You need a treat after your so-terrible shock this afternoon. Poor little one – to fall into the water like that, to be nearly drowned, to . . ."

"Well, I wasn't nearly drowned really, you know," said Claudine, a twinkle coming into her eye. "I knew I *shouldn't* be drowned, Aunt Mathilde, because Bobby and Mirabel were both in the water – and oh, wasn't it grand when I splashed that hateful woman from head to foot? I never guessed I would drench her like that!"

81

Mam'zelle's mouth fell open, and she stared at Claudine as if she could not believe what she heard.

"Claudine! Claudine! What is this that you are saying? Surely, no it is not possible – you could not have fallen on purpose! You would not be such a bad girl!" Poor Mam'zelle could hardly get the words out.

Claudine answered demurely. "On purpose, Aunt Mathilde! Why, how could you think of such a thing? Do you suppose that your niece could do a so-shocking thing as that? But how wonderful that it should happen just by Angela's mother! Ah, truly, that was a miracle!"

With a wicked twinkle in her eye, the unscrupulous Claudine walked off to get herself ready for going out. Mam'zelle stared after her. Ah, this Claudine – she was a bad, bad girl – and yet what a good, good girl she was too, to throw herself into the water in order to splash and punish an unkind woman, some one who had hurt and puzzled her aunt! Mam'zelle sat down on a hall-seat, feeling quite breathless. Which *was* Claudine – a bad girl or a good one? For the life of her Mam'zelle could not decide.

Meanwhile all the girls and their parents had gone off in their different cars. Angela had rolled away in her magnificent car – but a very quiet and subdued Angela. Somehow things had not turned out quite as she had planned. She hadn't shone in the reflected glory of her beautiful mother. She had only felt the scorn of the other girls because her mother had criticized their school in loud and complaining tones.

Angela looked out of the car-window and saw the happy faces of the twins, and saw Pauline walking with Mr. and Mrs. O'Sullivan. They were all going off together, chattering gaily.

"You all did *mar*vellously!" she heard Mrs. O'Sullivan say, in clear, happy tones.

Then she saw her friend Alison – and to Angela's enormous surprise, Eileen and Claudine were with her, all getting into a car together! Oh! How mean of Alison! Why hadn't she asked Angela to join up with her and her people? Fancy asking that common little sneak Eileen, and that awful outspoken niece of Mam'zelle's, Claudine! How *could* Alison do such a thing!

Angela did not think of what the real reason might be – a real feeling of kindness on Alison's part. She was angry and annoyed. She would show Alison exactly what she thought of her when she saw her next! If Alison wanted to make friends with charity-girls, let her – but she wouldn't have Angela Favorleigh, the Honourable Angela Favorleigh for her friend too!

There were two or three fairly big towns within easy reach of the school by car, and the different families chose their own town and hotel, and drove off. To Eileen's intense joy, Alison's mother chose to go to the town where Eddie lived!

"Oh," she said, as the car slid into the town. "This is where my brother lives. I wonder if I shall see him."

"Would you like to ask him to come and have dinner with us?" said Alison's mother.

Eileen shook her head. "Oh no, thank you. It's kind enough of you to ask *me* without asking *him* as well! But – if you wouldn't mind – I would love to slip along and see him after we've had dinner. His lodgings aren't very far from the hotel. He'd love to see me."

"Just as you like, dear," said Alison's mother. So they had their dinner, and a very good one it was, and then Eileen slipped off to see Edgar.

Claudine proved a great success with Alison's people. The French girl had naturally good manners, she was vivacious and amusing, and she was extremely pleased to have such a treat. Alison's parents really enjoyed the girl's company.

"Alison, I wish that French girl was your friend, and
83

not Angela," said her mother. "She really is nice. Don't you like her?"

"Yes, Mother, I do," said Alison. "She's quite different from us English girls, though – I mean, she hasn't our sense of honour – and honestly, she simply doesn't care *what* she does. But she's fun, quite sincere, and awfully kind."

"Here comes Eileen back again," said Alison's mother. "She must be very fond of her brother. She really looks happy now!"

Eileen did. Eddie had been delighted to see her. She beamed at Alison and Claudine in an unusually friendly manner. What a lovely day it had been!

Janet and the 'Stink-balls'

After the excitements of half-term the girls felt flat and dull. There didn't seem anything to look forward to now. Lessons were boring. The weather was too hot. It seemed a long time till the summer holidays.

"Janet! Bobby! Can't you think up some trick or other?" said Pat, with a yawn. "I wish you would. I shall die of boredom this week if something doesn't happen."

Janet grinned. "I've got rather an awful trick from my brother," she said. "I don't really know if we ought to play it, now we're fourth-formers."

"Oh, don't be an idiot!" said Doris. "Why can't we have a few jokes, even if we *are* fourth-formers! What's the trick?"

"Well – it's a perfectly frightful Smell," said Janet. "Wait a bit – I'll get the things."

She went up to her dormitory, rummaged about in one of her drawers and then came down again with a small box.

The others crowded round her. The box was full of what looked like tiny round glass balls, full of some sort of clear liquid.

"What are they?" said Pat, puzzled. "I've never seen them before."

"They are smell-balls," said Janet. "Stink-balls my brother calls them. When you break one and let out the liquid, it dries up at once – but leaves the most frightful smell behind."

"What sort of smell?" asked Doris, with great interest. "Like drains or something?"

"Well – like very bad eggs," said Janet. "My brother – he's simply awful, you know – he broke one of these balls at a very solemn meeting once, in our drawing-room at home – and in less than a minute the room was empty! You simply can't imagine what it was like!"

Bobby chuckled. "Let's break one in French class tomorrow," she said. "It's going to be terribly dull – translating pages and pages of that book Mam'zelle is so keen on – that French play. This trick is absolutely *sent* for things like that. Will you break one of these balls tomorrow, Janet, or shall I?"

"Well, you take one and I'll take one," said Janet. "Then if mine doesn't work – my brother says they are sometimes disappointing – you can use yours. See?"

The whole class were thrilled about the 'stink-balls'. Every one but Eileen knew about them. The girls were afraid of telling Eileen in case she sneaked to Matron, and the secret was found out. So Eileen was not told a word. She was astonished to find that so many of the girls hurriedly stopped talking when she came up, and then began chattering very loudly about quite silly things. She was sure they had been talking about her, and she felt hurt.

"If they're going to be beastly to me, I shall tell Mother, and they'll all get dozens of stockings to mend!" thought Eileen, spitefully.

Janet and Bobby went into the French class the next day with the little 'stink-balls' in their pockets. The lesson was just before Break.

"We'd better not choose any lesson except one just before Break," Janet had said, "because if the smell goes on too long, it might still be there in Miss Ellis's class, and I bet she'd smell a rat."

"She'd smell much worse than a rat once she sniffs one of your 'stink-balls'," said Bobby, with a grin.

"You see, we can open all the windows and doors and let the smell out well during Break," said Pat. "There won't be anything of it left by the time Maths. lesson comes afterwards with Miss Ellis."

The class were standing politely and silently when Mam'zelle came in. She beamed at the girls.

"Sit! Now today we will go on with this play of ours. I will allot the parts. You, Janet, can take the part of the old servant; you, Alison . . ."

The girls opened their books, hiding their grins as best they could. A trick performed by Janet or Bobby was always fun, great fun! The girls remembered the many other tricks the two had played, and chuckled. This would liven up a dull French lesson very considerably.

"Janet, will you please begin?" said Mam'zelle, amiably. She liked this fourth form. They were good, hard-working girls – and her dear little Claudine was there too, her face buried in her book – the good, good little girl!

Janet began reading in French. Her hand stole to her pocket. The girls behind her saw it, and tried to choke back their giggles. That was the worst of playing a trick – you always wanted to begin giggling far too soon, and it was terribly difficult to stop real giggles. Doris

86

gave one of her sudden snorts, and Mam'zelle looked up in surprise.

Doris turned it into a long cough, which set Mirabel off into giggles too. Mam'zelle glared at Mirabel.

"Is it so funny that the poor Doris has a bad cough?" she inquired.

This seemed funnier still to Mirabel and she went off into more helpless giggles which began to infect the others. Janet turned round and frowned. She didn't want Mam'zelle to suspect too soon that she was playing a trick. The others caught her warning look, and became as serious as they could again.

The lesson went on. Janet slid the little glass ball out of her pocket. Her hand was behind her, and the girls saw her press firmly on the tiny glass ball. The thin glass covering broke, and the liquid ran out, drying almost as soon as the air touched it. The liquid disappeared, and the tiny fragments of thin glass dropped unheeded to the floor.

After a few moments a curious smell drifted all round. Doris coughed. Alison sniffed loudly and said 'Pooh!'

It was a horrid smell, there was no doubt about that. It smelt of bad eggs, drains, dead rats, old cats' meat . . . all that was horrid!

Mam'zelle did not smell the smell at first. She was astonished at the sudden outburst of sniffing and coughing. She looked up. She saw expressions of disgust on every one's face, mixed with the desire to giggle.

"What is the matter?" demanded Mam'zelle, suspiciously. "Why do you pull these faces? Alison, stop saying 'Pooh!' Janet, why do you look so disgusted?"

"Oh, Mam'zelle – can't you smell it?" said Janet, an agonized expression on her face.

"Smell *what*?" said Mam'zelle, exasperated. The smell had not drifted her way as yet.

87

"Oh, Mam'zelle – the *smell*!" chorused half a dozen voices.

Mam'zelle looked puzzled and angry. She took a few enormous sniffs of the air, which made Doris explode into laughter.

"I smell no smell," said Mam'zelle. "This is a silly trick, yes. Stop sniffing, Janet. If you say 'Pooh' again, Alison, I will send you out of the room. Claudine, do not look like a duck that is dying."

"But, Aunt Mathilde, the smell, the smell! *C'est abominable!*" cried Claudine, who detested bad smells, and looked as if she was about to faint.

"Claudine! You too!" rapped out Mam'zelle, who, safely away at the end of the room, had not even got so much as a sniff of the evil smell yet. "Now listen, *mes enfants* – one more mention of a smell, and I fetch Miss Theobald herself here to smell it! It is all pretence. You are bad children."

This was a truly terrible threat! Miss Theobald would certainly be able to smell the smell as soon as she got into the room, and then there would be a big row. The girls looked at one another in dismay. They put their handkerchiefs to their noses and tried not to sniff up the ghastly odour.

Mam'zelle began to read out loud from the French play. After a few lines, she stopped. Strange! She felt as if she too now could smell something. She took a cautious sniff. Was it a smell, or was it not? Nonsense! Strange and horrible smells do not invade classrooms all of a sudden. Mam'zelle took another breath and went on reading.

The smell stole round her. Mam'zelle could smell it quite distinctly now. She stopped reading again and sniffed wildly. Yes, there was no doubt about it, a perfectly horrible smell was in the room! The poor, poor girls – they had smelt it first – and she had not believed them.

Mam'zelle gave a gulp and a choke as the smell really took hold of her. She fished about for her handkerchief. The girls, divided between disgust at the smell and an intense desire to giggle at Mam'zelle's horrified face, stuffed their hankies into their mouths, making all kinds of most peculiar noises.

"Girls," said Mam'zelle, in a choking kind of voice, "girls, you are right. There is a terrible smell in here. What can it be?"

"A dead rat under the floor-boards?" said Doris, obligingly, removing her hanky from her mouth for a moment.

Mam'zelle gave a small shriek. Rats, dead or alive, gave her shivers all down her back.

"Perhaps a drain has burst outside the window," said Pat, speaking in a muffled voice. "I'll look."

She went to the open window and leaned out, taking in deep breaths of the pure air there. One or two others joined her, thinking it was a very good idea.

"Perhaps it will go away," said Mam'zelle, hopefully. "Open the door, Janet, and maybe it will help to clear the room of this evil odour."

Janet thankfully opened the door. This was an amusing trick to play – but it had its drawbacks!

The draught of air took a good strong dose of the smell over to Mam'zelle's desk. She gave a loud exclamation. 'Tiens This is terrible! We shall all be ill. Pick up your books quickly and we will finish our lesson in the garden. I will tell Miss Theobald and maybe she will have the boards up to seek for a rat that is quite dead."

All but Claudine were delighted to go out into the garden. Claudine did not know which was worse – the smell in the classroom, or the insects out-of-doors. She thought there was very little to choose between them!

Soon the girls were sitting in a nice shady part of the garden, giggling whenever they thought of the awful smell drifting round their classroom. The lesson was no longer boring or dull! The smell had made it a great success.

Mam'zelle kept her word and reported the smell to Miss Theobald. "Ah, Miss Theobald!" she said, "it is a smell truly unbelievable! Of dead rats and mice, of eggs that are bad, of drains that are broke! It came into our classroom whilst the girls were reciting their French lesson, and it spoilt the whole hour. We had to leave the room and go into the garden."

Miss Theobald was surprised to hear of such a very strong and disgusting smell. In all her experience of schools, she had never yet come across a smell that had driven a class from the room.

"I will go and smell it," she said to Mam'zelle. "If it is a dead rat, or bad drains, then, of course, we must have the smell seen to at once, this very afternoon. The smell will remain there, if those are the causes."

But, to Mam'zelle's great astonishment and to Miss Theobald's mild astonishment, not a trace of the smell remained. The two of them sniffed all round the room, but it smelt fresh and clean.

"Extraordinary," said Miss Theobald, gazing at Mam'zelle. "You are quite sure, Mam'zelle, that it *was* a strong smell, a really bad one?"

Mam'zelle was most indignant. What, the Head Mistress was doubting her word? Mam'zelle at once began to describe the smell all over again, this time making it a smell ten times worse than before. Miss Theobald smiled to herself. She knew Mam'zelle's indignant exaggerations by this time.

"Well," she said, "I won't have the floorboards up, or the drains inspected today -- maybe the smell will not return. If it does, Mam'zelle, kindly report it to me at once, please, so that I may smell it myself before it goes away."

"Yes, Miss Theobald," said Mam'zelle, and went to

the mistress's common room, full of the Smell and of its power in sending her class into the garden. Every one listened in astonishment. It didn't occur to any one but the first form mistress, Miss Roberts, that it might be a trick. But Miss Roberts had had much experience of Janet's jokes, and it did cross her mind to wonder if this could be one of them.

"Let me see, Mam'zelle," she said, thoughtfully, "Janet is in the fourth form, isn't she?"

"Yes," said Mam'zelle, "but what has that got to do with my smell?"

"Oh – nothing I expect," said Miss Roberts. "But – if I were you, Mam'zelle, if that smell appears again, you trot down to Miss Theobald AT ONCE. I think she may be able to find the cause of it without taking up any floor-boards and examining any drains!"

"Of course I shall report to the Head at once," said Mam'zelle, with dignity.

And the time came when she did!

Miss Ellis Plays A Trick Too

The girls had been really delighted with the success of Janet's 'stink-ball'. Whenever Eileen had not been in the room, they had chattered and laughed about Mamzelle's disgust and astonishment.

"All the same, we'd better not do it again," said Janet. "I have a sort of feeling that once would be a success, but that twice would be a failure! You can pull Mam'zelle's leg beautifully once in a while, but not all the time."

"If you do the smell again, I shall be sick and go out

of the room," said Claudine. "It is the worst smell I have ever sniffed."

"We won't do the smell again," promised Bobby. "But I tell you what we *will* do – we'll pre*tend* there is a smell, shall we – and get old Mam'zelle all hot and bothered expecting one – she'll sniff and snuff, and we shall die of laughing!"

"Oh yes – that's a good idea," said Janet. "Doris, you can start off about the smell again in tomorrow's French Grammar class."

Doris grinned. She could act that kind of thing very well. So the next day, when Mam'zelle was ensconced safely in her desk at the end of the room, Doris began her act.

There was a very nice smell in the room, for Alison, the girl doing the flowers for the classroom that week, had filled a big vase with white pinks, and they scented the room beautifully. The girls could smell them as they worked.

Doris began to sniff. At first she gave very little sniffs. Then she gave two or three bigger ones.

"Doris! Have you a cold?" said Mam'zelle, impatiently. "Are you a first-former, come to class without a handkerchief?"

"I've got a hanky, thank you, Mam'zelle," said Doris, humbly, and took it out.

Then Janet began to sniff. She screwed up her nose, sniffed, and looked all round. Bobby gave a chuckle and turned it into a long cough. Mam'zelle frowned. She did not like behaviour of this sort; it made her angry.

Then Pat began to sniff, and pulled out her hanky too. Soon the whole class, all except Eileen, who was not in the joke, were sniffing as if they had bad colds.

Mam'zelle gazed at the sniffing girls, exasperated. "What is all this noise? Sniff-sniff-sniff! I cannot bear it."

Doris put on an expression of disgust. Mam'zelle saw

it, and an alarming thought came into her head. Could it be that terrible Smell again?

"Doris," she said, urgently, "what is the matter?"

"I can smell something," murmured Doris. "Distinctly. It's very strong just here. Can't you smell anything, Mam'zelle?"

Mam'zelle couldn't, which was not at all surprising. But she remembered that before she could not smell the smell until after the girls. She looked anxiously at the class. They all seemed to be smelling it.

"I will report it at once," said Mam'zelle, and she left the room in a hurry.

"Crumbs!" said Bobby. "I don't know that we wanted her to go to the Head about it! I say – she shot off so quickly we couldn't stop her!"

Unluckily for Mam'zelle the head was out. Mam'zelle was annoyed and upset. Here was the Smell again, and no Miss Theobald to smell it, and to know that she, Mam'zelle, had not exaggerated last time!

Mam'zelle popped her head in at the mistress's common room as she hurried back to the classroom. Miss Ellis was there, correcting exercise books belonging to the fourth form.

"Mis Ellis – I regret to say that that terrible Smell is back again," said Mam'zelle. "It is abominable! I do not think you will be able to take the fourth form in your room next lesson."

She withdrew her head and hurried back to the fourth form. She went in, expecting to be greeted by a wave of the terrible Smell. But there seemed to be no smell at all. Very strange!

"Mis Theobald is out," said Mam'zelle. "Alas, she cannot smell our Smell. Neither do I smell it yet!"

It was good news that Miss Theobald was out! The girls felt cheerful about that. Doris spoke up at once.

"Don't worry, Mam'zelle. We know what the smell

was this time – quite different from last time. It was only these pinks!"

Doris picked up the big bowl of pinks, walked jauntily to Mam'zelle and thrust them under her big nose. Mam'zelle took a sniff and the strong and delicious scent went up her nose.

"So!" she said to Doris. "It was the pinks you smelt. Well, it is a good thing Miss Theobald was not in. She would have come to smell for nothing!"

There were a few giggles – and then, as the door opened, the girls fell silent, and looked to see if it was Miss Theobald coming in after all.

But it wasn't. It was Miss Ellis, who, curious to smell this extraordinary smell that Mam'zelle seemed continually to get excited about, had come to smell it herself. She stood at the door, sniffing.

"I can't smell anything, Mam'zelle," she said, surprised. Mam'zelle hastened to explain.

"I smelt nothing, either, Miss Ellis. It was the pinks the girls smelt. Doris has just told me."

Miss Ellis was surprised and most disbelieving. "I don't see how the girls could mistake a smell of pinks for the kind of awful smell you described to me last time," she said. "I am not at all sure I believe in that Smell at all."

She gave her form a glare, and went out.

Mam'zelle was indignant. Had she not smelt the smell herself last time? For the rest of the lesson the class had a very peaceful time, discussing smells, past and present, with their indignant French mistress.

After Break came geography, taught by Miss Ellis. She came into the room looking rather stern.

"I just want to say," she said, "that I shall regard any mention of smells, bad or good, as a sign that you want a little extra work given to you."

The class knew what that meant. "A little extra work" from Miss Ellis meant a good two hours extra prep. So

94

every one immediately made up their minds not to mention the world smell at all.

But a terrible thing happened in ten minutes' time. Bobby had quite forgotten that she still had her 'stinkball' in her pocket, left over from the day before. And, in sitting down rather violently, after going with her book to Miss Ellis, she broke the thin glass surrounding the liquid. Then, in a trice, the perfectly awful Smell came creeping round the classroom once more!

Doris smelt it. Janet smelt it. Bobby smelt it and put her hand at once into her pocket, desperately feeling about to see if she had accidentally broken the little 'stink-ball'. When she found she had, she gazed round, winking and nodding at the others, to tell them of the awful accident. Miss Ellis's sharp eyes caught Bobby's signs. So she was not really very surprised when she smelt the smell coming towards her. What a terrible smell it was!

Miss Ellis thought things out quietly. Evidently yesterday's Smell had been this same horrible one – and the one Mam'zelle had reported today, and which Doris had said was pinks after all, was nothing to do with the real Smell – just a silly joke played on Mam'zelle.

"But this awful Smell is the real thing again," thought Miss Ellis, "and, judging by Bobby's signs to the others, was a mistake. I don't think the girls would dare to play a trick like this on me. Well – I will just play a little trick on *them*!"

Quietly Miss Ellis wrote a few directions on the board. Then she turned and left the room, closing the door after her. The girls stared at the board.

"Page 72. Write down the answers.

"Page 73. Read the first two paragraphs and then rewrite them in your own words.

"Page 74. Copy the map there."

"I say!" exploded Doris. "She's gone – and we've got to stay here in this awful Smell and do that work.

Bobby, you absolute idiot, why did you break that stink ball?"

"It was an accident," said Bobby, most apologetically. "I sat on it. I quite forgot it was there. Isn't the frightful? Miss Ellis has smelt it, of course, guesses it a trick, and for punishment we've got to sit through the smell and work at our geography – and we simply daren't complain!"

"I am not going to sit in the Smell," announced Claudine, emphatically. She got up. "I feel sick. I go to be sick."

She went off, and she made such wonderful sick noises as she passed Miss Ellis in the passage outside that Miss Ellis said nothing, but let her go to the bathroom. Trust Claudine for doing what she wanted! No one of the others dared to leave the room.

They sat there, choking into their handkerchiefs, moaning over their fate, but not daring to scamp their work. At the end of the hour, when the smell had somewhat lessened, Miss Ellis opened the door.

She left it open. "You may go for a short run round the garden and back," she said. "Bobby, remain behind, please."

With a wry face Bobby remained behind whilst the others fled out gladly into the fresh air.

"I was the one who caused that terrible smell that time," said Bobby, at once. It was never any good beating round the bush with Miss Ellis – not that Bobby was given to that, anyway. She was a straightforward and truthful girl. "But it was an accident, Miss Ellis, really it was. Please believe me."

"I do," said Miss Ellis. "But it is an accident that is on no account to happen again. You have all had your punishment, so I shall say no more about it. But I want you to warn the fourth-formers that any future smell will result in quite a lot of punishment!"

A Birthday – and a Grand Idea!

"Isn't it gorgeous weather?" said Isabel to Pat. "Day after day we get nothing but sun and blue sky. I wish we could have lessons sitting in the swimming-pool!"

"The coolest part of the day is the night!" said Doris. "I should like to sleep all day and work all night in the cool night breeze."

"Last night I woke up and saw the moon shining in at the window," said Hilary. "I got up and looked out – I simply can't tell you how beautiful the country looked, all lit up by moonlight. I wished I could go for a walk – have a moonlight picnic all by myself!"

"I *say*!" said Bobby, at once, "a moonlight picnic! What an absolutely marvellous idea! Let's!"

"Oooh," said the others, staring at Bobby, really impressed by the unusual idea. "Golly – what fun!"

"Yes, it would be," said Hilary, "but – now that we're fourth-formers, do you think we *ought* to?"

"Oh, Hilary – don't be so pious!" said Janet.

"I'm *not*," said Hilary, indignantly. "That's a thing I've never been. Well – perhaps it wouldn't matter. We could picnic in the school grounds. Oh I *say* – let's picnic by the swimming-pool, and have a moonlight swim!"

"Better and better!" said Bobby, giving a whoop of delight. "Golly – that would be super! Look here – let's wait till full-moon night – that's two nights from now – and have it then. The pool would be brilliantly lit and we could have a gorgeous time."

97

"It's my birthday then," said Mirabel. "That very day. Oh, let's make it then, and I'd feel it was a birthday treat too!"

"Right," said Janet. "Now we'd better make plans quickly, because we haven't much time to get anything." She turned to the quiet and responsible head-girl of the form, Susan Howes. "Susan, you'll come, won't you?"

Susan nodded. She was a good and trustworthy girl, but she loved a bit of fun, and she could not see that there was any harm in a moonlight picnic.

"I'll go down to the town today with Hilary, and buy a few things," she said. "I'll leave word at the grocer's and the baker's that you will all go in at different times and fetch one or two things. Then no one will suspect anything – we shall just quietly return to school with small parcels!"

"Shall we tell Eileen or not?" said Janet.

"No, of course not," said Bobby. "I bet she'd split on us and tell her mother – and then we'd all get caught and everything would be spoilt."

"Well – it's a pity to leave Eileen out of everything like this really," said Pat, "but we can't risk being found out. And these midnight affairs *are* such fun!"

Mirabel was thrilled that it was her birthday that day! It would make it all the nicer. She and Gladys, her quiet little friend, talked and talked about it.

"I'll take my birthday cake, of course," said Mirabel. "I'll save it up till then. Mother said she would send sixteen candles separately, and we'll stick them on the cake in their holders, and light them in the moonlight!"

Eileen was by now used to the others planning things without her. She knew that the tricks they whispered about together were not told her beforehand because she was known as a sneak. So she did not prick up her ears at all when she saw the girls talking together in low tones.

"What do I care for their silly tricks?" she thought.

98

"If they want to act like that, let them!"

So she did not try to overhear or find out their fresh secret. She went her own way, looking rather pale and unhappy. She rarely smiled now, kept herself quite to herself, and did not try to make friends with any one. She had been nice to Alison after the half-term treat, and Alison had benefited by her kindness by having no mending of her own at all to do ever since! But she still struggled with Angela's darning, though Angela was never very grateful.

Mirabel's birthday came. As usual her form gave presents. Some were small presents, if the girls had little money left, some were extravagant, like Angela's.

Angela gave Mirabel a book of very expensive music that she wanted. It cost twenty-one shillings and Mirabel was really quite overcome. "You shouldn't spend so much money on a birthday!"

"Why not?" said Angela. "My grandfather sent me five pounds last week. What's the good of having money if you don't spend it?"

Pauline, not to be outdone, gave Mirabel a music-case of fine leather. Mirabel was amazed. It was not usual to have such beautiful presents for a school birthday. She had not even known that Pauline had noticed that her own old music-case had a broken strap and was almost worn out.

"Oh, Pauline – this is beautiful!" said Mirabel, red with surprise and delight. "But you shouldn't do it. It's bad enough for Angela to do it – and for you to give me something so extravagant too, well really, I feel quite overwhelmed!"

"If Angela can do it, I can as well," said Pauline, a little stiffly. That took the pleasure out of the gift somehow, thought Mirabel. If Pauline only gave her something fine just because she didn't want to be outdone by Angela, well, there wasn't much kindness or affection behind the gift!

Claudine surprisingly gave Mirabel a very pretty bag. Claudine was one of the girls who had very little money, and said so – so Mirabel was really touched to have such a nice gift from her.

"Oh, thank you, Claudine," she said. "It is really lovely. But it's too extravagant of you! I know you don't have much pocket-money."

But Claudine seemed to have plenty that week! She bought eight pounds of cherries as her share of the picnic's goodies, and they came to ten shillings. Every one thought it was decent of her.

"Ah, when I have a little money, I like to spend it," said Claudine. "It is nice to spend. I wish I could spend always. That would be fine, to be like Angela and to say, 'I will have this, I will have that!' "

"Yes – but it does mean you don't have many treats, real *treats*," said Gladys. "I mean – if Mother and I save up for ages to go a good holiday together, it means much more to us and is a greater treat than any holiday could possibly be to Angela – who can have expensive holidays whenever she likes. To have a lot of money doesn't mean that you get more enjoyment than those who haven't much."

"Quite right as usual," said Isabel, giving the quiet Gladys a little pat. "Well, I wish I and Pat could buy more for this picnic, but it was our Granny's birthday last week and we spent most of our money on that mauve silk scarf we sent her. So we're cleaned out for a bit. I hope you won't turn up your nose at our birthday offering, Mirabel – it's only two drawing pencils with your name on!"

"That's very decent of you," said Mirabel, who really did not mind whether gifts cost ten shillings or ten pence. "I think you're all decent to me, every one of you. Everybody has given me a present."

Even Eileen had, though with many apologies for the poorness of her gift. "It's only a little hanky," she said to Mirabel. "And I'm afraid it's not even new. It's one of my own, but please take it, Mirabel, with my birthday wishes. I don't want to be the only one not giving you anything! You know I have hardly any pocket-money, and it's Eddie's birthday soon and I'm saving every penny for that."

Every one knew that Eileen had less money than any girl in the school. Her mother was mean over pocket-money. Certainly she had to work hard for her own money, but she seemed to think that the sixteen-year-old Eileen could manage on a penny or two a week, just as she had managed when she was a small six-year-old.

"I wish we could ask Eileen to go with us tonight," said Mirabel. She was usually a thick-skinned girl, who had little feeling for any one else, except for her friend Gladys – but she had been touched by Eileen's little gift, and her honest confession of having no money.

"Well, we can't," said Bobby, decidedly. "I know she told her mother that Janet said that there seemed to be more torn sheets in the fourth-form dormitories than in the whole of the rest of the school put together – and poor Janet has done oceans of mending this week. But who can help thinking our sheets are torn on purpose? On purpose to give us work to do! They were never torn like this before. Why, I could go a whole term without having to mend a pillow-case or sheet at all when our old Matron was here!"

"All right. We won't ask Eileen," said Mirabel. "I don't really care. She *is* a dreadful sneak, I suppose."

Everything was prepared in readiness for the moonlight picnic and swim. They sky was clear when the girls went to bed that night. They went to bed in the daylight, for the evenings were very long just then.

"There won't be any darkness at all, I should think," said Bobby, looking out of the window. "When daylight begins to go, the full moon will come swimming up the sky, and then everything will be almost as bright as day again. Golly, isn't it hot? I shall adore being in the water at midnight!"

Luckily for the girls, Eileen was a very sound sleeper. Once she was asleep, nothing ever seemed to wake her, and even when the fire-practice alarm had gone once in the middle of the night, she had not awakened. So the girls felt sure she would know nothing.

It was too hot to sleep! Some of the girls dozed off, and Eileen and Mirabel slept soundly. But the others tossed and turned, half-asleep and half-awake. So, when the big clock on one of the towers struck half-past eleven, there was only Mirabel to wake!

Eileen slept in a bed by the door of one of the fourth-form dormitories, and the girls had to tip-toe past her. But she did not stir. She had looked rather pale and tired lately, and now she slept very deeply. The girls had on bathing-suits under their dressing-gowns, and rubber shoes on their feet. They made no sound as they stole down the corridors, went down the stairs, and came to the big cupboard where they had hidden their food and drink.

With giggles and whispers they loaded themselves with the goodies, and then undid the garden door as quietly as they could. They left it a little open so that they could get in easily when they returned. There was no wind to bang it shut.

Keeping in the cover of the trees, the line of excited girls made its way towards the swimming-pool. How gorgeous the still water looked, lying calm and deep in the brilliant moonlight. The moon was now up, and was flooding the grounds with cold, silver light. Everything could be plainly seen. Only the warm colours of day-light were missing.

"We mustn't make too much noise," said Janet. "Our voices would carry a good way on a still night like this, I only hope no one will hear the splashing of the water

The excited girls made their way towards the pool

when we go in! Let's go in first, before we eat. I'm so hot."

Off came the dressing-gowns. Bare long legs gleamed in the moonlight. One after another the girls dived in or jumped in – all but Claudine, who had steadfastly refused to come in a bathing-suit, but had on her night-gown under her dressing-gown. The little French girl liked the excitement of the midnight picnic, but, hot though it was, nothing would persuade her to go into the water! She would throw herself in to punish a spite-ful-tongued woman – but she certainly would not go in for pleasure!

She stood and watched the girls, laughing. She glanced away from the pool – and suddenly saw a figure slipping silently between the trees. Whoever could it be?

Claudine Deals with Matron

Claudine ran quietly in her rubber shoes to see who was out in the grounds that night, besides the fourth-formers. It was Eileen! Eileen, whom the girls had left sound asleep in bed.

"The sneak!" said Claudine to herself. "She comes to peep and pry at us, and then she goes back to her so-severe mother to tell a tale! J will follow her back."

But somehow she missed Eileen, and could not see where she had gone. Claudine rushed back to the pool and almost fell into the water in her excitement at tell-ing the others what she had seen.

"Oh blow!" said Bobby, climbing out, the moonlight shining on the silvery drops running down her legs. "I suppose that sneak of an Eileen will go straight off to Matron – and before we can have anything to eat, she'll be here scolding us and rowing us and sending us back in disgrace."

"I will go back to the school, and keep watch," said Claudine, eagerly. "I know where Matron sleeps. I will go outside her door and stand there till I know for certain that either she is coming here, or that Eileen has not told tales after all."

"Right," said Bobby. "Hurry! And be sure to race back and warn us if you hear Matron dressing or wandering about. We simply mustn't be caught. But oh, what a shame if we can't have the moonlight picnic. And I bet Matron will confiscate Mirabel's lovely cake!"

Claudine sped off in her rubber shoes. She did not see Eileen at all. She went in at the open garden door and ran quietly up the stairs to the corridor at the end of which Matron slept.

She stood outside Matron's door and listened. There was not a single sound from inside. She could not hear either Eileen's voice or Matron's. On the other hand, she could not hear slight snores or heavy breathing. Claudine stood there, wondering what to do. *Had* Eileen seen the picnickers? *Did* she mean to tell tales? Where had she gone?

Then Claudine's quick ears caught a sound from inside Matron's room. The bed was creaking! Plainly Matron was awake. The bed creaked a little more, and then there came the sound of some one shuffling into slippers.

"Now she puts on a dressing-gown," thought Claudine. "Now she ties the girdle. But why is she getting up just now, if Eileen has not been to tell her?"

The little French girl squeezed herself into a dark corner as Matron's door suddenly opened. The thin narrow-shouldered figure appeared framed in the doorway, full in the moonlight. Matron looked rather grim.

She set off silently down the passage and turned off in the direction of the dormitory belonging to the fourth-formers. Claudine followed her like a moving black shadow, keeping cleverly in the dark corners. Matron went into the dormitory where Eileen always slept.

"Eileen!" said Matron, in a whisper. But there was no answer. Then Matron evidently patted the bed and found no one there. There came an exclamation, and Matron switched on the light. In a moment she saw the empty beds!

She went into the next dormitory, where the fourth-formers also slept, and again switched on the light. No girls there!

"Where are they?" said Matron, angrily. "I will not have this sort of thing! Why didn't Eileen warn me of this? She ought to know better than to join in tricks of this sort!"

Claudine heard these muttered words, and was surprised. So Eileen *hadn't* warned her mother! She had followed the others out, and must be hiding somewhere in the grounds, watching the fun.

And now Matron was going to spoil everything. Why should she? Claudine felt a sudden and intense dislike for the severe and spiteful Matron. There was no harm in a moonlight swim and picnic! Quite likely if the girls had asked Miss Theobald's permission, she would have laughed and granted it, just for once! And now Matron was going to interfere.

Matron went down the stairs. She came to the cupboard where the girls had stored their picnic food and drink. They had left the door open. Matron gave an angry exclamation and went to shut it.

And it was then that the Great Idea came to Claudine! It was an idea that might have occurred to any angry girl, but only Claudine would have carried it out.

Matron suddenly got the shock of her life! Some one

106

gave her a violent push so that she landed inside the cupboard, among old lacrosse sticks and tennis-rackets. Then the door was shut – and locked!

Matron was a prisoner! Claudine took the key out of the cupboard and put it into her dressing-gown pocket. Choking with laughter she ran out of the garden door and made her way to the swimming-pool. She could hear Matron hammering on the door. But the little back-hall beyond the garden-door, near the cupboard, was seldom used, and far from any sleeping-quarters. It was quite likely that no one would hear Matron at all.

"Now we are safe!" thought Claudine, triumphantly. "What a fine joke! But will these English girls think it is a joke?"

For the first time a doubt came into her mind. She, Claudine, knew it to be a grand, grand joke to lock that so-detestable Matron up in a dark cupboard, to stop her from spoiling the fun – but would the others think like Claudine? Might not this curious 'honour' they were always talking about prevent them from thinking it a joke? Might not Susan Howes, fourth-form head-girl, think it her duty to go and rescue Matron? One could never tell what the English would think to be right or wrong!

"Then I shall not tell them what I have done!" thought Claudine, as she sped along to the pool. "If they do not know, they cannot worry. Now I will only tell them that it is all right, Eileen has not told tales, and that Matron is quite, quite safe."

The girls climbed out of the pool and surrounded Claudine when she came running back.

"It's all right," said Claudine. "Very much okay. Eileen has not told tales. She is not back at the school. And Matron is quite, quite safe!"

"Oh *good*!" said all the girls, and shook the water from themselves. "What about some eats now?"

107

"Where's Eileen then, if she isn't in bed and didn't go back to school?" said Bobby, puzzled.

But nobody knew and nobody cared. Let Eileen wander where she liked so long as she didn't spoil their fun. And how good that Matron was safe too!

The girls were very hungry after their swim. They sat down to enjoy the food. There was bread, butter, potted meat, tins of sardines, marmalade, apricot jam, cherries, biscuits and Mirabel's big birthday cake. The candles did not show up very well in the bright moonlight, but still, it was fun to light them.

The girls had their picnic by the edge of the water, dangling their legs in the pool. The water was lukewarm, for the sun had warmed it thoroughly. It was simply lovely. There had never been such midnight fun as this!

"This cake is gorgeous," said Bobby, eating an enormous slice. "My word – I don't ever remember feeling so hungry. Are those sardine sandwiches? Pass them along, Susan."

Claudine enjoyed her meal more than any one. True, she was not so hungry as the others, for she had not been in for a swim – but she could not help thinking of Matron shut up in the dark cupboard, quite unable to spoil the fun of the fourth-formers! And that gave a very keen edge to her enjoyment of the picnic. She felt no anxiety as to what would happen when Matron was let out. Claudine never let things like that worry her at all!

The meal was over at last. Every scrap was finished. Even Angela said she had enjoyed it. Alison had not enjoyed it quite so much as the others because she had fallen into the water in her dressing-gown, and was worried as to how to dry it before Matron saw it. Mirabel said she had never enjoyed a birthday so much in all her life.

108

"It's been a great success," said Janet, pleased. "Now we'd better go back. Hark – there's one o'clock striking – Dong! Golly, I'm tired now."

Every one was tired. The swim had been rather strenuous, for there had been a lot of good-humoured racing and teasing. The girls cleared up crumbs, cartons, and paper-bags, and put empty ginger-beer bottles into a locker up in the gallery, meaning to collect them when it was safe.

"That's all, I think," said Susan, looking round. "Isn't the water lovely, gleaming in the moonlight. I just hate to leave it!"

But they had to leave the gleaming pool. They made their way back through the trees, whispering together. They came to the garden door, which was still open.

And then they heard a most peculiar noise. Bang, bang, bang, knock, knock, knock!

"Crumbs! What's that!" said Susan, startled.

"Let me out, let me out!" cried a muffled voice, and somebody kicked against a wooden door.

Alison and Angela were terrified. "It's a burglar!" said Alison, and tore up the stairs as fast as ever she could. Angela followed her, trembling.

Claudine pushed the others towards the stairs quickly. "Don't stop," she whispered. "Get back to the dormitories as quickly as you can. Don't stop. I will explain everything."

In the greatest astonishment the girls went upstairs to their dormitories. They crowded into the one in which Claudine slept, and demanded to know what the explanation of the curious noises was.

"It's Matron," said Claudine. "She's locked in that cupboard."

There was an amazed silence.

"*Who* locked her in?" said Bobby at last.

"I did," said Claudine. "She came into our dormitories and saw we weren't there. I did not want her to spoil your fun – so I pushed her into the cupboard and locked her in. Was I not quick and clever?"

An Infuriated Matron

For a minute or two no one said anything at all. The girls found it simply unbelievable that Claudine should have done such a thing. Locked Matron into a games cupboard! Left her there, shouting and hammering! Really, the French girl must be completely mad.

"No, I am not mad," said Claudine, reading their thoughts. "It was the only thing to do, wasn't it? She would have spoilt your fun, and I could stop her. So I stopped her."

"But Claudine – you'll get into the most fearful row!" said Janet at last.

"That matters nothing," replied Claudine, and certainly she acted as if she did not mind what happened! She was not in the least excited or upset. The girls went on staring at her, hardly able to take in the fact that Matron had been, and still was, a prisoner downstairs.

Then an awful thought came to Bobby. "Who's going to let her out?"

Nobody said anything. Not even Claudine wanted to set free a woman who would be sure to be violently and spitefully angry. But certainly she could not be left in the cupboard till the morning.

"Where's the key?" said Janet. Claudine produced it from her dressing-gown pocket. It was a large key. Claudine put her finger in the hole at the top of it and swung it thoughtfully to and fro.

"As I was the one who locked her in, I will also be the one to let her out," she said at last. "But I shall unlock the door very, very quietly, then open it a tiny way, and then I shall fly up the stairs, taking my heels with me."

The girls couldn't help smiling. "You mean, you will take to your heels and fly upstairs!" said Bobby. "You do say ridiculous things, Claudine. Honestly, I can't imagine how you dared to do such a thing – locking Matron into a cupboard – golly, it's unheard of! Why didn't you tell us what you had done, when you came back to the pool and joined the picnic?"

"I thought you would say, 'Ah, it is not honourable to do such a thing,'" explained Claudine. "I thought maybe Susan would feel she ought to go and set Matron free. So I said nothing."

"I never met any one quite like you before," said Pat. "You do the most awful things for perfectly good reasons! I mean – you throw yourself into the pool when you *hate* the water, just to punish some one who's been unkind to your aunt – and you go and lock Matron up into a cupboard just so that we shan't have our picnic spoilt! I must say you do the most dramatic things – we never know what you're going to do next!"

"Well – what are we going to do about Matron?" demanded Susan, who was getting worried. "Shall we let Claudine let her out?"

"I go," said Claudine, and got up with much dignity. She loved moments like this, when she took the stage and every one looked at her. She was not at all conceited, but there was to her a very satisfying feeling in doing something unusual and dramatic.

She went. The girls scrambled into bed, feeling that very shortly Matron would come bursting into the dormitories like an angry bull!

Claudine crept downstairs to the little back-hall by the garden-door. Matron was still shouting and hammering. Claudine slipped along to the door and put the key quietly into the key-hole – but just as she was about to turn it and unlock the door, she heard the sound of quiet footsteps on the gravel path outside!

She darted up the stairs at once, without turning the key. Let whoever it was coming by unlock the door! They would be sure to hear Matron, and set her free. Then she, Claudine, could get away in safety!

The footsteps came to the garden-door, and then some one slipped inside. It was Eileen! She stood still in the greatest astonishment as she heard the muffled cries and the banging on the door of the games cupboard.

"Why – it's mother's voice!" said Eileen out loud, in the very greatest amazement. "Where is she? She can't be in that cupboard!"

But she was, as Eileen very soon realized. The girl turned the key at once and opened the door. Matron stumbled out, almost beside herself with rage. She caught hold of Eileen in a fierce grip, not seeing what girl it was. Eileen cried out in pain.

"Mother! Don't! It's me, Eileen, However did you get into that cupboard?"

"*You!*" cried Matron, and let go Eileen's arm. "What are *you* doing here? Where have you been? How dare you go out at night like this? Tell me what you have been doing, at once!"

Eileen said nothing at all. Her mother gave her a shake. "You've been out somewhere with the fourth form. They are all out of their beds! What have you been doing? I shall report you all to Miss Theobald. Why didn't you tell me what was happening?"

"I can't say anything, Mother," said Eileen, in a frightened voice. It was news to her that the fourth form had been out that night. She had not noticed any empty beds when she had slipped out herself. She had not heard any noise from the swimming-pool either.

She had been out to meet Eddie her brother in the lane, and she was not going to tell her mother this. She no longer dared to meet him in the daytime, for she felt that any one might see her, and report her. So she had been meeting him once a week in the middle of the night, when all her dormitory was sound asleep.

Nobody knew this. And certainly she must not let her mother know, or Eddie would get into trouble too. What had the fourth-formers been doing? How mean of them to go off on a spree at night and leave her out! Somehow or other she must make her mother think she had been with them.

"You won't say anything?" said her mother in a threatening voice. "Well, tell me this – who locked me in here? I can't imagine that *you* would dare to!"

"Of course I didn't," said Eileen. "And I don't know who did, either. Carlotta might have. It's the kind of thing she would do. I really don't know, Mother. Please let me go back to bed!"

But Matron was far too angry and humiliated to let the matter drop. She swept up the stairs to the fourth-form dormitories, and switched on the lights. The girls all pretended to be asleep. Matron walked into the dormitory where Eileen slept, and spoke in a loud and angry voice.

"It's no good your pretending to be asleep. I know you're not. I've come to find out who locked me into that cupboard! I insist on knowing, here and now. That girl will be expelled from St. Clare's!"

Susan Howes sat up and looked at the angry Matron. "We all take the blame for that," she said, quietly. "We are very sorry, Matron, and we hope you will accept our apologies."

Matron made a fierce explosive noise. "Accept your apologies! Of course I don't! You won't get out of this as easily as that! I insist on knowing who locked

113

me in. Otherwise I shall go straight to Miss Theobald, here and now, in the middle of the night."

Claudine sat up in bed, ready to speak. She did not in the least mind owning up. But Bobby laid a warning hand on her shoulder, and pulled her over towards her, to whisper into her ear.

"Don't own up to Matron! She will go to your aunt too, and make a fearful fuss, and there's no reason why Mam'zelle should be brought into this. You can tell Miss Theobald yourself tomorrow if you want to."

"*Bien!*" said Claudine, snuggling down into bed again. "Very good! I do as you say, Bobbee."

Matron stood glaring round the room. Then she stamped heavily with her foot and almost shouted. "All right! I shall go to Miss Theobald. You will all have to explain what you were doing in the middle of the night, leaving your beds like that – and I warn you, I shall show no mercy on the person who has not owned up to locking me in. Eileen, get into bed. I am absolutely ashamed to think that a daughter of mine should have joined in midnight wrong-doing, and should refuse to tell me anything about!"

She went off down the corridor, walking angrily. The girls sat up.

"Whew!" said Bobby, "what a volcano! I say, Eileen, where were you? Does your mother really think you were with us?"

"Yes," said Eileen, in a low voice. "Please don't give me away. I was only meeting Eddie, my brother. I was afraid to tell my mother that, so I let her think I was with you. I didn't know what you had been doing, so I couldn't possibly tell her, of course, and that has made her very wild with me. We're all going to get into a most fearful row."

"I bet Miss Theobald won't be too pleased at being wakened up at this time of night," said Janet, looking at her watch. "It's half-past one! We'd better try and get some sleep – thought I expect the next thing will be Miss Theobald coming in and demanding explanations too!"

The girls tried to settle down and go to sleep. Mirabel fell asleep first, and then one by one the others did . . . all except Eileen, who lay awake, staring into the dark, worried and unhappy. Everything was going wrong! Everything was getting worse! Oh dear, she did hope the girls wouldn't give her away and say she had not been with them that night. They might quite well sneak about her. She had done plenty of sneaking that term, and it would not be at all surprising if they got a bit of their own back!

Matron walked down the corridor and made her way to the seperate wing in which the Head Mistress, Miss Theobald, had her set of rooms. She knocked loudly on the bedroom door.

"Come in!" said a startled voice, and there was the sound of a light being switched on. Matron opened the door. Miss Theobald was sitting up in bed, eyes heavy with sleep.

"What is the matter?" she said anxiously. "Is some one ill, Matron?"

"No," said Matron, her thin face still purple with rage. "Something much worse than that!"

"Good gracious, what?" asked Miss Theobald, hurriedly getting out of bed and reaching for her dressing-gown. "Quick, tell me!"

"It's the fourth form," said Matron, in a grim voice. "All out of their beds, every one. Even my Eileen. Goodness knows what they were doing!"

Miss Theobald sat down on her bed in relief. "Oh!" she said, "a midnight feast, I suppose? I thought you had come to report something really serious! Couldn't this have waited till the morning, Matron?"

"Indeed it couldn't," said Matron, "and for a very good reason, too. Somebody locked me for hours into the games cupboard in the back-hall by the garden-door!"

Miss Theobald stared at Matron as if she really could not believe her ears. "Locked you into the cupboard?" she said at last. "Are you quite sure? I mean – I really cannot imagine any of the fourth-formers doing that."

"You don't know half that goes on in the school," answered Matron in a grim and righteous tone. "Not half! My Eileen tells me most things, and you'd be surprised if I told you some of them."

"I don't think I want to hear," said Miss Theobald, "and I can't help thinking it is a mistake, Matron, to encourage Eileen to tell tales to you. Also I think you need not worry whether I know all that goes on or not. That is my concern."

Matron sensed the rebuke in Miss Theobald's words, and she began to feel angry that the Head had not expressed more anger and concern over her imprisonment in the cupboard. She looked grimmer than ever.

"Eileen set me free," she said. "Otherwise I might have been in the cupboard till the morning. A fine thing to happen to the Matron of a school like this! I went up to the fourth-form dormitories at once, and there were all the girls pretending to be asleep. Little hypocrites!"

"Oh, Matron, don't be quite so vindictive!" said Miss Theobald, feeling rather shocked at the Matron's tone. "You have never been Matron in a girl's school before, and you are not yet used to the mischievous ways of the various forms. But as a rule there is little harm in them. Who locked you in?"

"The girls won't say," said Matron, angrily. "But I demand that whoever locked me in should be expelled, Miss Theobald. A girl that does a thing like that is a very bad influence on the others!"

"Well, I expect they were all in it," said Miss Theobald. "I should never expel a girl without a much stronger reason than mere mischief, Matron. I am certain that the whole form shared in the fun, and you would not expect me to expel the whole lot, would you? Do try and see things in a reasonable light. You are angry and annoyed now – you will not be so inclined to want girls expelled in the morning."

"Aren't you coming back to the dormitories with me to demand who it was that locked me in?" demanded Matron, furiously, as she saw Miss Theobald taking off her dressing-gown and slippers.

"The girls will, I hope, be asleep by now," said the Head, getting into bed. "I see no reason for waking them all up again. This can easily wait till the morning."

Matron was infuriated. She had planned a most dramatic return to the dormitories with Miss Theobald, and had gone so far as to hope that the Head would demand to know the culprit and announce her expulsion there and then. She bit her thin lips and glared at Miss Theobald so angrily that the headmistress began to feel annoyed.

"Please go now, Matron," she said. "We will continue this rather complicated conversation in the morning."

Matron took a step forward, and her face took on a malicious look. "Well," she said, "I wasn't going to tell you till I'd found out the thief – but there's somebody in the fourth form who's been stealing, Miss Theobald! I've missed money – yes, and stamps too – and all kinds of things like notepaper and envelopes. You've got a nasty little thief in the fourth form, and I shall want *that* matter cleared up too! Otherwise, I am afraid – I shall go to the police!"

Miss Theobald disliked Matron intensely at the moment. It was quite plain that she took a real pleasure in saying these poisonous things.

"I think all these things must wait till the morning Matron," said the Head. "I will go into them thoroughly then. We can do nothing satisfactory tonight. Good night."

Matron walked out of the room without answering. She hoped she had given Miss Theobald a shock. She had not meant to talk about her missing money, for she was taking a great pleasure in trying to track down the thief herself – and then she had meant to take her by the shoulder and lead her triumphantly to Miss Theobald. Matron hoped that the thief and the one who had locked her into the cupboard were one and the same. She felt certain they were. Surely only a very bad character could lock her into a cupboard!

"We shall perhaps get to the bottom of things tomorrow!" she thought, as she got into bed. "I'll make Eileen tell me all that the fourth form did. I shan't say anything about my missing money to her, though, in case she warns the fourth form and the thief isn't caught."

The fourth-form girls woke up tired and sleepy and rather fearful the next morning. Had Matron been to Miss Theobald? What was going to happen?

Matron appeared at breakfast, grim and stern. Eileen had tear-stained eyes. Her mother had scolded her and demanded to know what the fourth form had been doing the night before. But Eileen had not told.

Bobby had spoken seriously to her. "Look here, Eileen – we didn't ask you to our picnic last night because we were afraid you'd sneak to your mother, as you often do. But we'll make a bargain with you. We will say nothing at all about your not being with us – Matron can go on thinking you *were* with us – but you in your turn aren't to give us away any more at all. See? And if you do, the bargain is automatically broken, and we shall tell on you. It's the only way to teach you that sneaking doesn't pay."

Eileen, looking pale and unhappy, had nodded. "Thank you," she said. "I couldn't bear Mother to know I go and meet Eddie. She would be so angry with him. I won't split on any of you any more. I've sneaked, I know – but it's so difficult not to answer Mother's questions sometimes."

Bobby guessed it was. Eileen had her own problems – but they wouldn't be solved by being weak and telling-tales! She had to find that out sooner or later.

But this morning Eileen had been determined and strong, for once, and had not answered Matron's insistent questions. Her mother had been very angry, and had even boxed her ears hard. Matron had a fierce temper when she let herself go, and poor Eileen had had to bear the brunt of it.

"Claudine," said Susan, in a low voice at breakfast-time, "if you want to own up to Miss Theobald about locking Matron up, you'd better go immediately after breakfast. But if you don't want to own up, you needn't. We'll all stick by you, and ask Miss Theobald to hand out a punishment to the whole form. After all, we had a good time, because of you, and we none of us want you to be punished for something we would all dearly like to have done ourselves."

"Thank you, Susan," said Claudine, thinking that these English girls could be very nice and fair and generous. "But I shall go to Miss Theobald. I am not ashamed of what I did. She is a nasty woman, the Matron, and I shall tell Miss Theobald that it filled me with pleasure to punish her for some of the unkind things she has done this term."

"Well – do and say what you like," said Susan, thinking that Claudine would, all her life, quite probably do and say exactly what she liked! "And good luck to you!"

So Claudine went to the Head, knocked firmly at the door and went in.

She began without any beating about the bush, "Please, Miss Theobald, I have come to say that it was I who locked Matron in last night. I suppose it is not a thing that any English girl would have done, with their so-fine sense of honour, but I am French, and I did not like Matron, and I wanted the fourth form to have a good time. We went for a moonlight picnic, Miss Theobald, and swam in the pool. At least, I did not swim, but the others did, and they said it was magnificent."

Miss Theobald found it difficult not to smile at the frank confession. Claudine always had such a very charming and innocent air, even when she was doing, or owning up to the most extraordinary things. The Head looked keenly at the intelligent French girl.

"Why do you dislike Matron?"

"You wish me to say the truth to you?" asked Claudine. "Well, then, I will say this. Matron can find out, through Eileen, all the little stupidities and mischiefs of the fourth-formers, and then, see what happens! Miraculously our sheets get torn and we spend hours mending them. Suddenly stockings are full of holes, vests are without buttons. Alas, Miss Theobald, we do not all like Eileen, and if we show it, then these unhappy things happen, and we sit indoors mending, whilst others play games."

"I see," said Miss Theobald. She had suspected this. "Claudine, you cannot go about locking people into cupboards. I am certain that even French schoolgirls do not do this!"

"Ah, Miss Theobald, I do not go about always locking people up!" said Claudine, beginning to launch herself on to one of her long and involved speeches. "No, no – only those people who deserve it should be imprisoned into cupboards. Me, I would never . . ."

Miss Theobald thought that Claudine had many of Mam'zelle's own ways. She smiled to herself and stopped the voluble explanation.

"That will do, Claudine. You will please apologize to Matron this morning, and you will accept what punishment she gives you. There is one thing more . . ."

She stopped and looked keenly at Claudine. The little French girl listened intently, for she had a great liking and respect for the wise and kindly Head Mistress.

"That one thing more is about the English sense of honour," said Miss Theobald. "You speak lightly of it, even mockingly – but I think, Claudine, in your heart of hearts you see it for the good and fine thing it really is. When you go back to France, Claudine, take one thing with you – the English sense of honour."

Claudine looked solemn. She was very much moved.

"Miss Theobald," she said, "believe me when I say that I do not really mock at it. First I did not understand it. Then I thought it was tiresome in others and even more tiresome to have oneself. But now I begin to learn it, and it is good, very good."

There came a knock at the door and Matron came in, looked grimmer than ever. She meant to have things out with Miss Theobald at once. Claudine was simply delighted to see her. "Now," thought the clever girl, "now I will apologize to Matron in front of Miss Theobald, and she will not dare to be too spiteful to me nor to give me too great a punishment!"

So Claudine went meekly up to Matron, cast her eyes down to the ground, and spoke in a very timid voice.

"Matron, it was I who locked you in last night. I apologize to you and beg your forgiveness. I will gladly bear what punishment you give me!"

Miss Theobald looked on with much amusement. She knew that Claudine was acting a part, and had cleverly taken advantage of Matron's coming, to apologize at once, in front of the headmistress herself.

Matron went purple in the face. She glared at Claudine and scolded her severely.

"You're a very naughty girl! You deserve to be expelled! And what is more, I *would* have you expelled if it was not that your aunt is the French mistress here, and it would break her heart to have a thing like that happen."

Actually Matron was afraid of Mam'zelle, who was apt to fly off into even more violent tempers than Matron herself. Matron even felt that Mam'zelle might come and scratch her face and pull her hair out if she dared to try and get Claudine expelled.

"It is good of you to consider my kind aunt," replied Claudine, still in a very meek voice. "What is my punishment to be?"

"You will spend every hour of your spare-time this week helping me to mend the school linen," said Matron. She did not see the flash of joy in Claudine's downcast eyes. Ah, now she would be able to get out of games and walks for a whole week! "Very well, Matron," she said, putting on a most miserable voice, that did not deceive the listening Miss Theobald in the least. She turned to the Head.

"I will return now to my class," she said, and gave Miss Theobald a brilliant and grateful smile. She went out of the room, shutting the door quietly. Miss Theobald thought that no one could help liking the naughty little girl, clever as she was at always getting her own way!

"Well, Miss Theobald," said Matron, in a war-like tone, "can we get down to this business of stealing? I can't have it happening any longer. It's got beyond me. Day after day it happens. And what's more, some more of my money has gone since last night! Only two shillings, it is true – but stealing two shillings is as bad as stealing two pounds. It's thieving, right down bad thieving. And I think the girl who does it ought to be expelled. You wouldn't agree to expelling the girl who locked me in last night – but maybe you'll have to, Miss Theobald! Yes, maybe, you'll have to!"

"What do you mean?" asked Miss Theobald in surprise.

"I mean this," said Matron, "I think it's that little French girl who's taking things! She's always in and out of my room with mending – and I hear she's been throwing a lot of money about lately – and *I* know she hasn't much, because Mam'zelle herself told me. So maybe, Miss Theobald, you will find that it's best to get rid of a girl of that sort, and will agree with me that it would be a good thing to expel her!"

Pauline's Mother

Before Miss Theobald could make up her mind that day what would be the best way to tackle the Matron and her accusations, a nasty accident happened in the gym.

It happened to Pauline. She was climbing one of the

ropes, and somehow slipped and fell to the ground. She fell with one leg doubled up under her, and there was a sickening crack.

Pauline crumpled up on the floor, went very white, and then quietly fainted. The games-mistress hurried to her in alarm, and Matron was at once called and the doctor telephoned for.

"Broken her leg," he said. "Clean break. Nothing to worry about."

He set it, and Pauline was put to bed, still white from the shock. Miss Theobald went to see her, and Pauline looked beseechingly up at her.

"Don't tell my mother," she said. "I don't want to worry her. Please don't tell her."

"My dear child, I have already telephoned to her," said Miss Theobald in surprise. "Why shouldn't she be told?"

"I don't want to worry her," said Pauline, faintly. "Please ring her up again, Miss Theobald, and say she is not to worry, and of course she is not to bother to come and see me. Say I will write to her today."

"You can't write today," said Miss Theobald gently. "You must keep absolutely quiet today. I will ring your mother up again this evening, and tell her not to bother to come and see you if she cannot do so."

"Tell her *not* to," said Pauline. "She – she –hasn't been well, you see. I don't want her to be worried."

Every one was sorry about Pauline. The girls were not allowed to go and see her that day, but they sent her in little gifts of flowers and fruit and books.

"Everything seems to be happening at once," said Bobby. "I say – wasn't that a perfectly awful talk that Miss Theobald had with us this morning?"

It had been a very serious and solemn talk indeed, and had happened just before dinner that morning. All the fourth-formers, except Pauline, who was in the sanatorium, under Matron's care, had been called to Miss Theobald's drawing-room.

The Head had lightly touched on the night before, telling them that Claudine had confessed, and had apologized to Matron and received a punishment for her extraordinary behaviour. She said that she would have given permission herself for a moonlight picnic and swim if she had been asked, but she realized that girls as young as the fourth still thought it was more fun to do things with*out* permission, than with.

This made the more responsible ones squirm a bit. They did not like being considered young and silly. Then Miss Theobald passed on the Matron's other complaint. This was very much more serious, of course, and the fourth form listened in great discomfort as the Head told them that a thief was in their midst, and must be found out, or must come and confess.

"You must realize that what would be a small thing, comparatively speaking, in the lower school, among the younger children, is a much more serious thing among you older girls," said the Head, "and Matron is quite rightly concerned about the matter. Whoever is taking things from her room is doing it deliberately and continually – it is not something done in a moment of urgency and perhaps regretted bitterly afterwards – it is, apparently, quite cold-blooded, frequent and deliberate."

The girls talked about it all afterwards, the affair of Matron being locked up in the cupboard taking second-place to this much more serious accusation. Who in the wide world could it be?

"Matron is certain it's some one in the fourth form because our common room is the only one near to her room," said Bobby. "It would be easy for some one to slip out now and then, see if the coast was clear, and then pop into Matron's room and sneak something."

"Such queer things have been stolen besides money,"

said Janet, puzzled. "Stamps – and notepaper and envelopes. Why those? Matron says that biscuits and sweets have been taken too. It almost looks as if somebody has been taking anything they could, just out of spite."

"Well, we none of us love Matron!" said Bobby, grinning. "If it was just a question of paying her out for her meanness, any one of us might be the culprit!"

"I am glad such things happen to her," said Claudine. "She deserves to have unhappiness, because she gives so much sadness to others. The poor Eileen has red eyes all day long today!"

"Yes, I can't help feeling sorry for her," said Doris. "It's bad enough to have Matron as Matron, but to have her as mother as well must be pretty awful!"

Pat, Isabel, Janet, Bobby and Hilary discussed the matter between themselves on the tennis-court that day.

"Who *could* it be?" said Bobby.

"Has any one suddenly been having more money than usual?" wondered Pat. The same thought at once came into every one's mind.

"Yes – Claudine has. She's been splashing it about like anything!"

"And she has plenty of chance of going into Matron's room because she is always taking mending there!"

"But it *can't* be Claudine! It's true she hasn't our sense of honour – but she wouldn't do a thing like that!"

"You know she doesn't care *what* she does when she dislikes somebody or wants to get even with them. She wouldn't think it was wrong, even."

The five looked at one another, suddenly feeling extremely uncomfortable. They knew Claudine had very little money indeed – and yet she had given Angela that lovely bag – and had spent ten whole shillings on cherries for the picnic. It did really seem as if it might be Claudine.

The bell rang for tea-time and the girls sped into the school. After tea Angela and Alison went off together down to the town to get something they wanted. On the way back they overtook an elderly woman, dressed in sober black clothes, sensible flat-heeled shoes, and a plain hat. She wore glasses, and her face was thin and worn, but kindly.

"I bet that's a cook come after the job at St. Clare's," said Angela to Alison. The girls passed her and she turned and spoke to them.

"Could you tell me if I am on the right road for St. Clare's? You are St. Clare girls, aren't you?"

"Yes," said Alison. "Keep straight on."

The girls made as if to go on, but the woman stopped them with a question that astonished them very much.

"How is my girl Pauline now? The Head Mistress telephoned me to say she had broken her leg this morning, and I caught the first train I could. I'm Mrs. Jones."

Angela and Alison stopped dead in the road and stared open-mouthed at the little elderly woman. They remembered Pauline's wonderful stories of Mrs. Bingham-Jones, her beautiful and wealthy mother. They simply could not understand this plain, tired-looking woman, almost old, being Pauline's supposedly wonderful mother.

Scorn welled up at once in Angela's heart. So Pauline, who was always trying to out-do and out-boast Angela herself, had, for a mother, a woman who looked like a worn-out cook. She tried to pull Alison up the road quickly.

But something in Mrs. Jones's tired face had touched Alison. Alison had many faults, but she was sensitive to other people's feelings, and she could sense Mrs. Jones's worry and anxiety. She shook her arm away from Angela's.

"Pauline is all right," she said, kindly. "We couldn't

127

see her today but we've all sent her something — you know, flowers and books and things — just to cheer her up. Are you better now? Pauline was *so* disappointed that you and her father couldn't come and see her at half-term, because you were ill."

Mrs. Jones looked extremely surprised. "I haven't been ill," she said. "I wanted to come at half-term, but Pauline wrote to say there was a case of scarlet-fever at the school, and the half-term matches had been put off, so would I not come."

Alison was horrified. In a flash she saw that Pauline, afraid that her mother would not shine among the other mothers, knowing that she had told all kinds of lies that would be found out when the girls saw her elderly, tired mother, had actually made up the lie about scarlet fever to stop her people from coming at half-term — and had pretended to be bitterly disappointed because they weren't coming!

Angela, of course, heard what was said, and an expression of scorn and contempt came over her face.

"*Well!*" she said, "there was no case of ..." But Alison was not going to let Angela interfere in the matter. She gave her friend a sharp nudge that made her squeal in surprise. Then she gave her such a fierce look that Angela said no more, but thought in surprise that Alison must be mad to treat her, Angela, like that.

"I hope Pauline is happy at St. Clare's?" said Mrs. Jones. "She has always wanted to go there, ever since she heard about it. I didn't see that I could afford to send her, but I managed to scrape enough together. Her poor father is an invalid, you know — has been for years — but I expect she's told you all that. We haven't a lot of money, but I did want Pauline to have a good time at a nice school. I said to her, 'Well, my dear, you won't have as much pocket-money as the others, and you won't have as many treats, but there you are, if you like to go under those conditions, I won't stop you.' "

128

Mrs. Jones talked to Alison, not to Angela. She liked Alison's pretty, kindly little face, and was glad to have some one to talk to. Angela gave a snort of contempt, and went quickly on, up the hill towards St. Clare's.

"It's quite a way, isn't it?" said Mrs. Jones, beginning to pant. "I didn't take a taxi, because taxis are expensive and I thought I could easily walk. Poor little Pauline – it is terribly bad luck to have broken her leg like this. I thought she would be so pleased to see me, if I can hurry along at once."

Alison didn't feel so certain. She thought that if Pauline had kept her mother away by lies at half-term she would certainly not want her at St. Clare's now, with all her lies exposed for what they were.

"Pauline is disgusting," thought Alison. "She really is. She takes everything from this poor little mother of hers, who probably goes without a lot of things she wants in order to pay for Pauline here – and then keeps her away from the school because she is ashamed of her! Beast!"

Alison took Mrs. Jones to the school door and left her there in charge of a maid. She went to take off her hat and blazer and joined the rest of her form in the common room.

"I hope Angela doesn't go and hold forth about Pauline's poor old mother," thought Alison uncomfortably. "I feel sorry for the old thing. She looked so tired and worn."

She heard Angela's voice as she opened the common-room door.

"And my dear, I know who it was that took Matron's beastly money and everything! There's not a doubt of it. It was Pauline!"

"Pauline! What do you mean? Why do you say that?" came Janet's voice at once.

"I'll tell you why," said Angela, and paused dramatically. "I and Alison walked up the road with Pauline's mother today – and from what she said to us it's pretty certain that our dear Pauline is a frightful story-teller and quite likely a horrid little thief!"

Angela – and Claudine

"You'll have to tell us why you say all this," said Bobby. The whole of the fourth form crowded round to hear. Only Claudine was not there, and neither, of course, was Pauline.

"Well, listen," said Angela, spitefully, "I and Alison were walking up the road and we saw an ugly little elderly woman, awfully plain, dressed in black in front of us. I thought she must be a cook coming to try for the job going here. And it turned out to be Mrs. Jones, Pauline's mother – not Mrs. *Bingham*-Jones, if you please, but just plain Mrs. Jones."

"She's a nice little woman," said Alison, not liking the contempt in Angela's voice.

"*Nice* little woman!" said Angela, rounding on Alison scornfully. "Common as dirt, you mean! And when I think of Pauline's airs and graces – trying to make out her mother was as good as mine – trying to pretend that her family were as grand as mine really are – swanking about her cars and things – and they're as poor as church mice, and can only just afford to send Pauline here! Golly, won't I tell Pauline what I think of her when I see her! *I'll* tell her what I think of dear Mrs. Jones, dressed up like a cook, moaning about her poor little Pauline."

Before any one else could speak, Alison stood up.

130

She was rather white, and there was a queer look on her face.

"You won't tell Pauline anything of the sort," she said. "You won't tell Pauline *anything* that's going to make her ashamed of that poor old mother of hers. Don't you realize how you'll make her hate her mother, if she knows you saw her and are saying this kind of thing about her? I think Pauline has behaved disgustingly about things, but I'm not going to have you making matters worse for Mrs. Jones by saying horrible things about her to Pauline."

Angela was amazed. Could this be her friend Alison talking to her like this? She stared at her, unable to say a word. Then she found her tongue.

"Well, if you stick up for people like Pauline's awful mother, I'm jolly glad you're not coming to stay with me for the holidays," she said, spitefully. "I'm going! I shan't stay here to be insulted by somebody I thought was my best friend."

Poor Alison was now trembling, for she hated rows. Angela moved towards the door. But to her intense surprise and annoyance, two girls caught firmly hold of her arms and sat her down violently, almost jerking the breath out of her body.

"You may not want to listen to Alison, but you're jolly well going to listen to *us*!" said Carlotta, her gypsy eyes flashing fire. "Now *we* will say a few things!"

"Let me go, you beasts," said Angela, between her teeth.

"You seem to be talking a lot about mothers," said Carlotta, bending over the angry Angela, and talking in such a fierce tone that Angela drew back, afraid. "Well, we *will* talk about mothers – *your* mother! We would not talk about her if it was not necessary – but it is very necessary now, in order to get some sense into your thick head!"

131

"You're jolly well going to listen to us!" said Carlotta

"I'll scream if you don't let me go," said Angela, in a rage.

"Every time you scream I shall slap you hard, like that," said Carlotta, and gave Angela such a smack on her plump shoulder that she squealed in pain.

"Shut up, Carlotta," said Bobby. "You can't act like that."

"Yes, I can," said Carlotta, coolly. And Angela knew she could, so she made no further sound.

"Pauline's mother may be tired and old and plain and poor," said Carlotta, "but that's no reason to despise her. Now there *is* reason to despise *your* mother, Angela! She is a spoilt, rude, discontented, horrible little snob – just like you are! And will you please tell her on no account to come here again, turning up her nose at everything, because we don't want to see her, we dislike her and despise her, and we want her to take you away as soon as ever she will!"

"Hear hear!" said Bobby, Janet and the twins. Angela went very pale. These were terrible things to hear, but she had brought them on herself. She too, had been ashamed of her spoilt mother when she had come at half-term – but she had not guessed how bitterly the girls had resented her contemptuous attitude towards the school and all it stood for.

"That's enough, Carlotta," said Susan Howes, uncomfortably. And it was enough. Angela looked as if she was about to faint. She wanted to sink through the floor. She, who had boasted and bragged of herself and her family, who set herself up as better than any of them, was being spoken to as if she were dirt. She gave an enormous sob, and fled from the room.

"Well, thank goodness she's gone," said Pat. "Cheer up, Alison. I was proud of you when you spoke up like that. Perhaps now you will see Angela as clearly as *we* see her."

"Yes – I do," said poor Alison, really distressed. "I

133

think she's awful. I did feel so sorry for that poor Mrs. Jones – and Angela had nothing but scorn for her. There's no kindness in her!"

"None at all," said Janet. "Well – she's got to learn that kindness breeds kindness, and spite breeds spite. She'll have an awful time if she doesn't."

"Do you think it's right, what Angela said, that Pauline might be the thief?" said Doris. "She *has* splashed money about very much lately – and if she's really poor – where did it come from?"

"We half thought it might be Claudine," said Isabel. "You know, she's poor too – hardly ever has a penny – and then, quite suddenly she had lots of money. And you know how unscrupulous Claudine is! I like her – but she simply has no sense of honour at all! We did wonder if it could be her."

"Sh! Sh!" said some one. But too late – for Claudine, who had come in unnoticed, had heard what Isabel had said!

The little French girl at once pushed her way to the front of the crowd of girls. Isabel saw her coming, and was horrified. Not for the world would she have had Claudine hear what she had said!

"Claudine!" she said, "I'm sorry you heard. Don't be angry. We only thought it because you seem so different from us in your ideas of honour. And it did seem to us that if you disliked Matron, you might pay her out in that way."

Claudine looked round the little group, intense anger in her small face. She saw Isabel's earnest face, Pat's scared one, Bobby's watchful one – and then, to the enormous astonishment of the listening girls, the anger in her face melted away – and Claudine threw back her head and laughed!

The girls stared at her in surprise. Honestly, thought Doris, you simply never know what Claudine will do!

Bobby thought how like Mam'zelle she was, in her

swift changes from anger to laughter. But what a blessing that Claudine could see any humour in Isabel's words!

"I am not angry," said Claudine, at last, wiping away the tears of laughter. "No, I am not angry. You English girls, you are so serious and solemn and so very, very honourable. I too have my own honour, and although it is not quite like yours yet, perhaps, one day it will be. The good Miss Theobald, she said to me this morning that one thing I must take back to France with me, one only – the English sense of honour."

"Just like Miss Theobald to say a thing like that," said Janet. "But why did you laugh just now, Claudine?"

"I laugh because I was thinking so suddenly of the reason why I have so much money now to spend," said Claudine, smiling her infectious smile. "But first, if I tell you, you must promise, on your English honour, that never, never will you tell my Aunt Mathilde what I have done!"

"Oh, Claudine – *what* have you done?" said Pat, imagining the most awful things.

"You remember my so-beautiful cushion-cover that my aunt loved so much?" said Claudine. "Well, I sold it to one of your mothers for quite a lot of money! You see, I needed money – there were birthdays coming, and I do not like to have so little. And one of your mothers, she was so nice to me, and she bought my so-beautiful cover, and I sent it her by post. I explained to her that it was my own, and I lacked for money, and she was so, so kind to me."

"Was that *my* mother?" asked Alison, suspiciously. "I saw you talking nineteen to the dozen to her at half-term. Mother *would* do a nice thing like that, and never say a word about it. I hope she puts the cushion-cover in my bedroom, that's all!"

"Well," said Claudine, grinning all over her little

135

monkey-face, "it *might* have been your so-nice mother, Alison. My sense of honour forbids me to say. And now I appeal to *your* sense of honour also, not to tell my aunt what has happened to my cushion-cover. I told her I had sent it to my mother."

"You *are* an awful story-teller, Claudine," said Gladys, shocked. "You deceive people right and left! I just can't understand you. Why couldn't you tell Mam'zelle you had sold the cover, instead of telling lies and keeping it a secret?"

"Ah, me, I adore secrets!" said Claudine, her eyes dancing. "And Aunt Mathilde would have written to the so-kind mother and got the cover back and repaid the money, and I should have been so, so sad, for it is nice to earn money, do you not think so?"

"I think you're a puzzle," said Janet. "I'll never make you out, Claudine. You go and tell lies in order to sell your cushion-cover and get money for somebody's birtday – you shut Matron up to give us a good time – you . . ."

"Ah, say no more of my badness," said Claudine, earnestly. "One day I may become good. Yes, certainly I shall become good if I stay at this so-fine school for another term!"

"Well, you're jolly decent not to have taken offence at what I said," said Isabel, warmly. "I'm glad you told us where you got the money from. I'm afraid now it means that Pauline must have taken it. She's had such a lot of money lately. Blow! I wish beastly things like this wouldn't happen! What do you think we ought to do about it?"

"Hilary and I will go to Miss Theobald and tell her everything," said Susan. "We can't tackle Pauline now, she won't be fit enough. But Miss Theobald ought to know what we think and why. Come on, Hilary. Let's get it over!"

Alison is a Good Friend

Hilary and Susan went to Miss Theobald's room and knocked on the door. She called out to them to come in. Fortunately she was alone. She looked up with a pleasant smile as the two girls came in.

"Well?" she said, "what do you fourth-formers want? You haven't been getting into any more trouble I hope?"

"No, Miss Theobald," said Susan. "But we are rather worried about this stealing business – and we have an idea who it is."

"Why doesn't the girl herself come to me, then?" said Miss Theobald, looking very serious.

"Well – she can't," said Susan. "You see – we think it's Pauline – and you know she's in the San. with a broken leg."

"*Pauline!*" said Miss Theobald, astonishment showing in her face. "I can't think it is Pauline. She isn't the type. No – surely it cannot be Pauline."

"We thought it might be Claudine at first," said Hilary. "But it isn't."

"Ah, I am glad of that," said Miss Theobald. "I still cannot think it is Pauline. She is not altogether sensible in some ways – but she did not seem to be at all a dishonest girl."

"Well, Miss Theobald, we have something else to tell you about Pauline, which will show you that she is really peculiar in some ways, and not at all truthful," said Susan, gravely. "We are not, of course, telling tales

137

to you – but we know we can't deal with this ourselves, so we have come to you."

"Quite rightly," said Miss Theobald, also very gravely. "Well – what is there to say about Pauline? Her mother is with her now, and possibly I might be able to have a talk with her about Pauline before she goes."

Hilary and Susan together told Miss Theobald of Pauline's ridiculous boasting and lying – of how she had put off her mother coming at half-term, by telling an absurd story about a scarlet-fever case – how she had pretended to be bitterly disappointed – how she had always seemed to have plenty of money, and yet her mother had told Alison she was afraid that Pauline would always be short of pocket-money.

"So, you see," said Hilary, "putting everything together, and knowing what an awful fibber Pauline was, we felt it was probably she who stole from Matron."

"I see," said Miss Theobald. "Curiously enough people who tell lies for the reason that Pauline tells them, are rarely dishonest in other ways. You see, Pauline lies because she longs to be thought better than she is – that is the *only* reason she lies. Now, if she stole, she would know herself to be despicable, and that others would despise her too. So she would not steal. But from all you tell me I am afraid that she does steal. Having so much money when it is clear that her mother cannot supply her with much, is very curious."

"Yes, it is," said Susan. "Well, Miss Theobald, we have told you all we know and think. We would all like this stealing business to be cleared up – the fourth form hate it, as you can imagine – and we are glad to leave it in your hands to settle."

There came a knock at the door. Miss Theobald called "Come in". Before any one entered she nodded to the two fourth-formers to dismiss them.

"I will see to everything," she said. "I will talk to Pauline – possibly tomorrow or the day after – as soon
138

as she has recovered from the shock of her broken leg. The doctor is to put it into plaster, and then she will return to school to do lessons, whilst it is healing. It is essential that I should have this matter cleared up before she returns to the fourth form."

A maid had entered the room and waited until Miss Theobald had finished speaking. "Please, Madam," she said, "Mrs. Jones would like a word with you before she goes."

"Tell her to come in," said Miss Theobald. Mrs. Jones came in. Hilary and Susan glanced at her curiously as they went out. So this poor, tired, worried-looking little woman, so plainly dressed, was Pauline's marvellous, pretty, beautifully dressed wealthy mother! What an idiot Pauline was!

Mrs. Jones plunged into her worries as soon as the door shut. "Oh, Miss Theobald, I'm really bothered about Pauline. She didn't seem at all pleased to see me. She cried her heart out when I told her I'd met some of her school-fellows on the way up, and had talked to them. I just can't understand her. I thought she'd be so pleased to see me. She even blamed me for coming – said I was making a fuss – and after all she's my only child, and very precious to me."

Miss Theobald looked at the distressed woman and was very sorry for her. She wondered whether or not to say anything about Pauline's stupid boasting, and to explain that Pauline's unkindness was because she was ashamed of having her lies exposed for what they were – she was ashamed of her mother, ashamed of not having enough money, ashamed of everything, so that she had forced herself to make up a whole new family and home of her own.

Then she decided not to say anything. It would only hurt and worry the poor little woman even more. She must have a serious talk with Pauline first, and perhaps she could persuade Pauline herself to put matters right.

So she listened, and tried to comfort Mrs. Jones as best she could. "Don't worry," she said. "Pauline has had a shock, through falling like that. Don't take any notice of what she says."

Mrs. Jones went at last, only half-comforted, feeling puzzled and hurt. Miss Theobald sighed. There suddenly seemed to be quite a lot of difficult problems to solve. How upset poor Mrs. Jones would be if she had to be told that her only child was a thief, as well as a stupid boaster!

"I will have a talk to Pauline tomorrow or the next day," thought Miss Theobald. "I only hope Matron does not make any more fuss – really, she is a most unpleasant woman."

Matron did make plenty more fuss! She went storming into Miss Theobald's room the next morning, with another complaint.

"Ten shillings gone this time! A ten-shilling note! Out of my purse too. And I had hidden it for safety in my work-basket. But it's gone all the same. Miss Theobald, that girl has got to be found and expelled!"

Miss Theobald listened in astonishment. How could *Pauline* be the thief if she was in the San. with a broken leg? But, as Matron went on complaining, it appeared that her work-basket had been in the San. She had taken it there to do her mending, as she had to sit with Pauline.

So Pauline *might* have been able to take the note from the purse. Other girls had popped in and out too, as Pauline was allowed to see her form that day. It was all very tiresome. Miss Theobald got rid of Matron as soon as she could, thinking that a lot of trouble was coming out of the fourth form that term!

The fourth-formers had been very cool towards Angela since the row. Angela looked pinched and unhappy but nobody felt sorry for her, not even Alison.

At half-past twelve Alison saw Angela putting on her hat to go out.

"Where are you going?" she asked. "You know we musn't go down to the town alone – do you want me to come with you?"

"No," said Angela, sulkily. "If you want to know what I'm going to do, I'll tell you. I'm going down to the nearest telephone box to telephone to my mother and tell her all the beastly things you've said about her, and ask her to come today and take me away!"

"No, don't do that," said Alison, distressed. "We only said those things because you were so horrid about poor old Mrs. Jones, Angela."

But Angela's mind was made up and off she went. Alison waited about miserably, not liking to tell the others. She pictured Angela's mother sweeping down in her Rolls-Bentley, spiteful and malicious, ready to say all kinds of horrible things about St. Clare's and its girls. It was not a pleasant thought.

Presently, about five minutes before the dinner-bell, she saw Angela coming back. But what a miserable, tear-stained Angela! Alison went to meet her, unexpectedly liking this humble, unhappy Angela far more than she had liked the bright and boastful one.

"What's the matter?" she said. Angela turned to Alison, and began to weep bitterly.

"Oh, Alison! Mother's away – and I got on to Daddy instead. But instead of listening to me and comforting me, he was very angry. And oh, he said Mother hadn't any right to talk as she did at half-term – and he was going to see *I* didn't grow up thinking I could say hurtful things to people – and he's coming today to see Miss Theobald about me!"

"Oh, Angela!" said Alison, in dismay. "How simply awful! He *must* have been angry. Miss Theobald won't be at all pleased when she hears you've been telephoning to your people and complaining. You'll get into a row from every one!"

"Oh, I know, I know," wept Angela. "I don't know what to do. Oh, Alison, I know I've been beastly. But please don't desert me now. I was awful yesterday about Pauline's mother. I'm ashamed of it now. Do, do be my friend again."

"Angela," said Alison, looking very serious all of a sudden, "I've been a very bad sort of friend to you. I've praised you and flattered you and thought the world of you, when all the time it would have been better to have laughed at you and teased you, like the others do. Bobby would have made you a much better friend, or the twins. They would have been sensible with you. I've spoilt you and been silly."

"Well, never mind, go on being my friend," begged Angela, who, now that things were looking black, felt that she simply *must* have some one who liked her. "Please do, Alison. I'll try and be nicer, I really will. But oh, what shall I say to Daddy when he comes this afternoon? I'm so afraid of him when he gets really angry."

"Listen," said Alison, "immediately after lunch we'll go down to the telephone box again. You get on to your father, and then say that you've been thinking things over, and you've come to the conclusion you've been an idiot but you'd like another chance. Then let me have a word with him, and maybe between us we can stop him coming."

"Oh, Alison, you're a brick!" said Angela, drying her eyes, and sniffing. "Daddy liked you. He'll listen to you. Oh thank you for your help."

The dinner-bell had long since gone. The two girls were late. Miss Ellis, taking a look at Angela's swollen eyes, contented herself with a few sharp words and then said no more.

Immediately after dinner the girls went off to the

telephone box. Angela got through to her annoyed father, and made her little speech. "I've been an idiot. I see it now. Don't come down, Daddy. I'm going to try and do better. Here's my friend Alison to talk to you."

The telephone receiver was passed to Alison, who, rather nervous, spoke the little speech she herself had prepared.

"Good afternoon! This is Alison speaking, Angela's friend. Angela is all right now. She was upset before, and rather silly. But I am sure she is going to settle down now and be a sport. So I don't think you need to leave your work and come to St. Clare's."

"Oh," said Angela's father, in a grim voice. "Well, as I'm very busy, I won't today. But any more nonsense from Angela and I shall come down and make a Big Row. I put Angela into St. Clare's because it's the finest school I know. And there she is going to stay until she, too, thinks it's the finest school *she* knows. If you really are her friend, you'll help her to realize this. You've been there some time, I know."

"Yes, I have," said Alison, earnestly. "And it is the very finest school in the kingdom! I'll teach Angela that, really I will, and so will the others."

"Well, don't spoil her," said the far-off voice, not sounding quite so grim. "Shake her up a bit! She may look like a golden princess, or an angel, but she's not a bit like one inside. And I'd like her to be. Tell her to speak to me again."

Angela took the receiver. What she heard comforted her. "Thank you, Daddy," she said. "I'll try. I really will. Good-bye."

She put the receiver back, looking much happier. "Daddy said that although he is often angry with me, he will always love me," she said to Alison. "And he said if I loved him, I'd try to be a bit more like he wants me

143

to be. So I shall try now. Thanks, Alison, for your advice!"

She squeezed her friend's arm. Alison took Angela's arm in hers and they walked back to the school. Alison was talking sternly to herself as they went.

"Now, no more telling Angela she is lovely! No more flattering her! No more praising her up to the skies because she looks like an angel! It's no good looking like one if you're just the opposite inside. Tease her and laugh at her and scold her and point out her faults – that's what I've got to do if I'm to be a real friend to Angela."

And, to the astonishment of all the fourth form, things between the two friends appeared now to be quite changed! Angela was now the docile one, accepting teasing criticism, and Alison was the leader!

"Good for both of them!" said Bobby, with a grin. "This will make Angela a nicer person altogether, and will end in giving Alison quite a lot of common sense!"

Matron has a Shock

"I wonder whether Miss Theobald has tackled Pauline about taking Matron's money and other things yet," said Hilary to Susan, after tea that day.

Eileen looked up, startled. She had not been there the day before when the matter had been discussed, and Hilary and Susan had gone off to see Miss Theobald. She had been cross-examined continually by her mother, who had tried to find out exactly what the fourth-formers had done on Mirabel's birthday night –

but Eileen had kept her word, and had not told her anything.

"Pauline – taking Mother's money?" said Eileen, amazed. "What's all this? I haven't heard a word about it."

"*Have*n't you?" said Janet, surprised. "Oh no – you were with Matron when we discussed it yesterday –and today we haven't had a minute to say anything about it. Not that there's anything much to say, really, except that we all think it's Pauline who has taken the things belonging to your mother. You see, we know now that her people can hardly afford to send her here and that she hasn't much pocket-money – so, as she has been splashing money about lately, we felt sure she was the thief. She's such a fibber, she could quite well go a bit further and be a thief as well!"

"And Miss Theobald is going to tackle her about it," said Susan. "Hilary and I went and told her everything yesterday. I'm sorry Pauline broke her leg – but really, if she's a thief as well as a story-teller, I think it's a good punishment for her."

Eileen sat and stared at the chattering girls. Bobby thought she looked rather strange.

"Do you feel all right?" she asked. "You look a bit funny."

"Of course I'm all right," said Eileen. She got up and went out. To the girls' astonishment they saw her, a minute later, flying down the drive at top speed.

"What's up with Eileen?" said Hilary, in amazement. "Has she forgotten we've got prep to do tonight?"

She apparently had. She did not turn up for prep at all, and Miss Ellis sent to ask Matron if she had kept Eileen with her for any reason. Matron appeared at the classroom door, looking annoyed.

"I can't imagine where Eileen is," she said. "I hope you will punish her, Miss Ellis. She has been such an obstinate, stubborn girl lately."

Eileen did not even return for supper, and it was only when the fourth-formers were getting undressed that they saw her again. Doris looked out of her dormitory window and saw Eileen coming up one of the school-paths. With her was somebody else.

"It's Eddie!" said Alison. "Gracious, won't Eileen get into a row! She must have shot off to see Eddie, and now he's come back with her."

Eileen looked strung-up and tearful. Eddie looked much the same. They disappeared into the school. Instead of going up to their's mother's room, they went straight to Miss Theobald's room.

"Cheer up!" whispered Eddie. "I'm here! I'll take care of you, Eileen."

The two went into Miss Theobald's room. The Head Mistress looked surprised to see Eileen with a boy. Eileen told her who Eddie was.

"This is my brother Edgar," she said, and then she broke down, and began to sob bitterly and piteously. Miss Theobald was distressed. Eddie put his arm protectingly round his sister.

"Don't cry," he said. "I'll tell about everything." Then he turned to Miss Theobald.

"Miss Theobald," he said, "today Eileen heard that another girl, Pauline, was going to be accused of stealing from Matron, our mother. Well – it was Eileen that took all the money and other things, not Pauline or any one else!"

"*Well!*" said Miss Theobald, thinking that surprises were coming thick and fast in the last few days. "But why? What made her do such an extraordinary thing?"

"It was because of me," said Eddie. "You see, I got a job in an engineering works at the beginning of this term, and Mother was very pleased. Well, I hadn't been there long before I had an accident with a car, and they sacked me. I – I didn't dare to tell my mother, Miss Theobald."

146

Miss Theobald looked at the weak, thin face of the lad in front of her, and was not surprised that he feared his bad-tempered, spiteful-tongued mother. How she would tear him and rend him with her tongue, if she knew he had failed in his job!

"Well," went on Eddie, swallowing hard, and still holding his arm round Eileen, "well, I thought maybe I'd be able to get another job fairly soon, and then Mother need only be told that I'd changed jobs. But, you see, I'd no money, and I had my lodgings and food to pay for — so I managed to hitch-hike over here one day and see Eileen without Mother knowing. And I asked her to give me what money she had."

"I see," said Miss Theobald, very grave. "And Eileen stole from her mother to give to you."

"I didn't know she was taking Mother's money," said Eddie. "I thought it was her own — out of her money-box or out of the post office savings. I knew she'd got a little. And she brought me biscuits too, and some note-paper and stamps to apply for other jobs. She's — she's been such a brick to me, Miss Theobald."

"Oh, Eddie, I'd do anything for you, you know that," sobbed poor Eileen. "But Miss Theobald, when I knew Pauline was going to be accused of something *I'd* done — then I rushed out and went to Eddie, and told him everything. And he came back with me to tell you. Oh, Miss Theobald, we don't dare to tell Mother!"

"What a mix-up!" said Miss Theobald, looking at the two scared, unhappy young faces before her. She could not help in her heart blaming Matron very much for all this. If she had been a kindly, loving mother, helping her children instead of expecting far too much of them, this would never have happened. They would have gone running to her for comfort and help instead of hiding things from her, and stealing from her, too frightened to do anything else.

"You see," said Eileen, drying her eyes, "as Eddie is

147

Mother's son, I didn't really think it was wrong to take her money and other things to help him."

"I see," said Miss Theobald. "But it *was* wrong all the same. Eileen, I am glad to think that you had the courage to realize that you could not let another girl bear the blame for your own wrong-doing. That is a great point in your favour."

There was a pause. Then Eddie spoke, rather nervously. "Miss Theobald – do you think you could see Mother for us? Please do. She might not be so terribly angry if you spoke to her first."

Miss Theobald felt a little grim. "Yes," she said, "I *will* see her. You two can wait in the next room until I have spoken to her."

Eddie and Eileen retired to the next room, looking forlorn and frightened. Miss Theobald rang her bell and told the maid who answered it to ask Matron to come and speak to her.

Matron soon appeared, crackling in starched apron and uniform.

"Sit down, Matron," said Miss Theobald. "I have found out who has taken your money and I wanted to tell you about it."

"I hope you will expel the girl," said Matron, in a severe voice. "After all, Miss Theobald, I've got a girl here myself, in the fourth form. It's not a very good influence for her, is it, to have a thief living side by side with her!"

"Well, Matron," said Miss Theobald, "I have made up my mind that I myself will not decide whether to expel this poor little thief or not. You shall decide, and you alone."

Matron's eyes, sparkled. "Thank you," she said. "You may consider that my decision is taken. The girl will go – and go tomorrow!"

"Very well." said Miss Theobald. "Now listen to my story, please. This girl did not steal for herself, but for some one she loved, who was in trouble."

"Stealing is always stealing," said Matron, in a righteous voice.

"She was afraid to go to her mother for help, afraid to go to her for advice," continued Miss Theobald.

"Then the mother is as much to blame as the girl," said Matron. "Mothers who have children so scared of them that they will steal have done a very bad job as mothers."

"I thoroughly agree with you," said Miss Theobald. "Neverthless, this girl had the courage to come and tell me, and she asked me to tell you."

"Where *is* the little thief?" said Matron, fiercely, "*I* shall have a few words to say to her, I promise you! Out she goes tomorrow!"

Miss Theobald stood up and opened the door connecting her drawing-room with her study. "You will find the little thief in here," she said. "With her brother."

Matron walked firmly into the study, ready to lash out at the thief. She saw there her two children, Eileen and Eddie. They stared at her nervously.

"What's this?" said Matron, in a faint voice. "Why is Eileen here – and Eddie?"

"Eileen is the thief, Matron – and Eddie is the one she stole for – and you are the hard mother they were too scared to come to for advice and help," said Miss Theobald, in a grave and serious voice. "And I think, knowing you as I do – that Eileen is not the one who should leave St. Clare's – but you!"

Matron's face suddenly crumped up and her mouth began to tremble. She stared unbelievingly at Eileen and Eddie. Eileen was crying again.

"You are a hard and spiteful woman," went on Miss Theobald's solemn voice. "This boy and girl need help and comfort, but they would never get it from you!"

"I've got another job, got it today, Mother!" said Eddie. "I shall pay back every penny Eileen took.

You're not to scold her. She did it for me because she loved me. Soon I shall earn enough money to let her live with me and keep house for me. Then you won't be bothered by either of us. We've always disappointed you. We weren't clever or gifted, though we did our best. But I'll look after Eileen now."

"Don't, Eddie, don't," said his mother, in a choking voice. "Don't talk like that. What have I done? Oh, what have I done to have this punishment on my shoulders?"

Miss Theobald shut the door. They must sort things out for themselves. Matron had made her own bed and must lie on it. Those two children would probably be all right because they loved each other and would always stick together. They were weak-willed and not very attractive characters – but their love for each other would give them strength and courage.

Miss Theobald took up the telephone receiver. She got through to the old Matron, who was now almost recovered from her illness.

"Matron?" said Miss Theobald. "Can you come back tomorrow? You can have as easy a time as you want to – but we can't do without you any longer! Yes – I have a feeling that the present Matron will be gone by tomorrow! Good – we *shall* be pleased to see you back!"

Things Settle Down At Last

And now still one more thing remained to be done. Pauline must be seen, and her affairs put right too. So accordingly next day Pauline was astonished to see Miss Theobald coming into the San. looking much more serious than usual.

It was the second surprise Pauline had had that day. The first was when quite a new Matron had appeared, plump and jolly and twinkling. Pauline had stared at her in astonishment, delighted not to see the other Matron.

"Hallo!" said this new Matron. "So you've broken your leg! Very careless of you. Don't make a habit of it, will you?"

"Where's the other Matron?" asked Pauline.

"She's had to leave in a hurry," said Matron, putting Pauline's bed-clothes straight. "So I've come back. And let me warn you I'm a Real Old Bear! I've been here for years and years, I'm probably a hundred years old, and I've scolded most of the girls' mothers as well as the girls themselves!"

"Oh, you're the old Matron the girls have told me about," said Pauline, pleased. "That's good! Why did Matron leave in such a hurry? Has Eileen gone too?"

"Yes," said Matron. "They both had to leave in a hurry. Not our business why, is it? Now then – what about those pillows?"

Pauline had hardly got over her astonishment at seeing a different Matron, when Miss Theobald came in.

As usual the Head went straight to the point, and soon the horrified Pauline was realizing that Miss Theobald, and the girls too, all knew what a stupid, untruthful boaster she had been.

She lay back in bed, feeling ashamed and miserable. Miss Theobald went relentlessly on, and finished by telling her how unhappy and puzzled she had made her mother.

"She came rushing to see you," said Miss Theobald. "She panted up from the station because she could not afford a taxi – and you know what sort of a welcome you gave her!"

Pauline turned her face to the wall and a tear trickled down her cheek.

"And there is yet another thing," said Miss Theobald, remembering. "Some one has stolen money – and because you seemed to have plenty, though the girls heard this week you were supposed to have very little pocket-money, *you* were suspected of being the thief! So you see, Pauline, to what big and terrible suspicions bragging and story-telling can lead us!"

"Oh! I've never stolen a thing in my life!" cried Pauline. "I had some money in the savings bank – and without Mother knowing I took my savings book here with me – and when I wanted money I took some out. That's how I had plenty of pocket-money, Miss Theobald. Please believe me!"

"I do believe you," said Miss Theobald. "But you must hand over your book to me and not withdraw any more money without your mother's permission. And, if you stay here at St. Clare's, you will have to do what some of the other girls do, who have very little money – say so quite honestly! Nobody minds. We should never judge people by the amount of money or possessions they have, but by what they *are*. You must learn that, Pauline, or you will never know what real happiness is."

"I feel very miserable," muttered Pauline, anxious for a kind word. "I – I don't know how I shall face all the girls after this!"

"Tell Susan or Hilary or the twins that you have been foolish," said Miss Theobald, getting up. "They are all sorry you have broken your leg, and I think they will see that you are treated kindly – but you will have to *earn* their kindness and friendship now, Pauline – not try to buy it with tales of wealth and great possessions! Earn their friendship by being sincere and natural and kindly. As for feeling miserable – well, that is part of the punishment you have brought on yourself, isn't it, and you will have to bear it as bravely as you can!"

Miss Theobald turned to go. She smiled down at Pauline, her smile kinder than her words, and the girl felt a little comforted.

She did as Miss Theobald had advised and confided in Hilary, when she came to see her. Hilary was outspoken but helpful.

"You're a frightful idiot, really frightful. And I shall only help you, and make the others decent to you on one condition, Pauline."

"What?" asked Pauline.

"That you write to your mother, and say you are sorry for being such a beast to her when she came to see you, and tell her you'll give her a great welcome next time she comes," said Hilary. "I'm not going round putting everything right for you, my girl, unless you first do a little putting-right yourself! And don't you dare to brag about a single thing more this term, or we'll all sit on you good and hard!"

And with that piece of advice, Hilary went off to tell the others that Pauline had come to her senses at last, and, as she had broken her leg, and was feeling pretty miserable, what about giving her a chance when she came back to class?

"Well, what with Eileen gone, and Angela reforming

herself fast, and Pauline getting a little sense knocked into her, and Matron disappeared for good, we seem to be getting on nicely!" said Bobby, with one of her grins.

"It only remains for Claudine to get the English sense of honour," put in Pat. "Then we shall indeed be a form of saints!"

Alison had a letter from Eileen the following week. She read it to the others.

DEAR ALISON,

I don't know whether you were ever told, but I was the thief. You see, Eddie was out of a job (he's got a good one now) and hadn't any money, so he asked me to help him and I did. But I hadn't much money myself, so I took Mother's, and some other things too.

Well, it was a most frightful shock to Mother, and she said she couldn't bear to stay at St. Clare's another day. So we packed and went. Miss Theobald was frightfully decent to Eddie and me. I simply can't tell you how decent. She even offered to keep me on at St. Clare's, when Mother went. But I couldn't face you all, and anyway I don't fit in there. I know I don't.

So I am going to study shorthand and typing, and then I am going to get a job in the office where Eddie works, and we shall be together. Mother is quite different now. I think it was an awful shock to her to find out how bad I was – but it was for Eddie, and I couldn't help it. Mother has been kinder and gentler. Really, you would hardly know her. Eddie and I think that when we are both earning money Mother won't need to work, and then she can take a rest and perhaps feel happier.

I thought I had better let you know what happened to me, because I left so suddenly. I left my silver thimble behind, in the school work-box – the one in the fourth-form cupboard. Will you please have it yourself in gratitude for taking me out at half-term, as I can never repay that?

I hope Pauline's leg is better. Please, Alison, don't always think unkindly of me, will you? I know I was a sneak, but you can't imagine how difficult things were for me sometimes.

Yours with gratitude,
EILEEN PATERSON.

The girls were all rather touched by this letter. Alison at once found the thimble and said she would wear it and not think too badly of Eileen.

"It was mostly her mother's fault she was such a little sneak and beast," said Bobby. "Golly, we're lucky to have decent mothers, aren't we?"

Angela went red at this remark but said nothing. She had been so much nicer lately – and she had determined that when she went home for the holidays, she was going to praise St. Clare's night and day, and not allow her mother to say a single word against it! Mothers could make bad or good children – "but," thought Angela, "maybe children could alter mothers sometimes too." She was going to have a good try to make her mother change her mind about quite a lot of things. Miss Theobald would have been very delighted if she had known some of the thoughts that went through Angela's golden head those days.

"Hols. will soon be here now," said Pat to Isabel. "It's been an exciting term, hasn't it – and aren't you glad our old Matron is back? Hie, Bobby – what about a really good trick to round off the term? Can't you and Janet think of one?"

"I dare say we can," grinned Bobby, her good-natured face looking tanned and even more freckled than usual.

"We could put a frog in Claudine's desk, or fill her

pencil-box with earwigs," suggested Janet with a wicked look at the horrified Claudine.

"If you do such a thing I take the train and the boat to France at once," declared the French girl.

"She would too," said Janet. "Well – perhaps we'd better not try out anything of that sort on Claudine. It would be a pity if she went back to France before she had had time to get that 'sense of honour' she is always talking about!"

Claudine threw a cushion at Janet's head. It knocked over Doris's work-basket. Doris leap up and threw a heap of mending at Claudine. It scattered itself over Mirabel who was just coming into the room. The girls shrieked with laughter to see Mirabel standing in surprise with somebody's vest over her head.

In a trice there was a fine fight going on, with squeals and yells. Arms, legs, and heads stuck out in all directions.

The door opened again and Miss Theobald looked in with a visitor.

"And this," she said, "is the fourth-form common room. Girls, girls, what *are* you doing? What *will* you be like as six-formers, if you behave like kindergarten children now!"

What will they be like? Not very different I expect! We'll wait and see.

THE ENID BLYTON TRUST
FOR CHILDREN

We hope you have enjoyed the adventures of the children in this book. Please think for a moment about those children who are too ill to do the exciting things you and your friends do.

Help them by sending a donation, large or small, to the ENID BLYTON TRUST FOR CHILDREN. The trust will use all your gifts to help children who are sick or handicapped and need to be made happy and comfortable.

Please send your postal orders or cheques to:

> The Enid Blyton Trust For Children,
> International House
> 1 St Katharine's Way
> London E1 9UN

Thank you very much for your help.

Enid Blyton's books have sold millions of copies throughout the world and have delighted children of many nations. Here is a list of her books available in paperback from Dragon Books.

First Term at Malory Towers	£1.50	☐
Second Form at Malory Towers	£1.50	☐
Third Year at Malory Towers	£1.50	☐
Upper Fourth at Malory Towers	£1.50	☐
In the Fifth at Malory Towers	£1.50	☐
Last Term at Malory Towers	£1.50	☐
Malory Towers Gift Set	£5.50	☐
The Twins at St Clare's	£1.50	☐
The O'Sullivan Twins	£1.50	☐
Summer Term at St Clare's	£1.25	☐
Second Form at St Clare's	£1.50	☐
Claudine at St Clare's	£1.50	☐
Fifth Formers at St Clare's	£1.50	☐
St Clare's Gift Set	£5.50	☐
Mystery of the Banshee Towers	£1.25	☐
Mystery of the Burnt Cottage	£1.25	☐
Mystery of the Disappearing Cat	£1.25	☐
Mystery of the Hidden House	£1.50	☐
Mystery of Holly Lane	95p	☐
Mystery of the Invisible Thief	£1.25	☐
Mystery of the Missing Man	£1.25	☐
Mystery of the Missing Necklace	95p	☐
Mystery of the Pantomime Cat	95p	☐
Mystery of the Secret Room	£1.25	☐
Mystery of the Spiteful Letters	£1.25	☐
Mystery of the Strange Bundle	95p	☐
Mystery of the Strange Messages	95p	☐
Mystery of Tally-Ho Cottage	85p	☐
Mystery of the Vanished Prince	95p	☐

To order direct from the publisher just tick the titles you want and fill in the order form.

Fiction in paperback from Dragon Books

Richard Dubleman
The Adventures of Holly Hobbie   £1.25 ☐

Anne Digby
Trebizon series
First Term at Trebizon   £1.50 ☐
Second Term at Trebizon   £1.50 ☐
Summer Term at Trebizon   £1.50 ☐
Boy Trouble at Trebizon   £1.50 ☐
More Trouble at Trebizon   £1.50 ☐
The Tennis Term at Trebizon   £1.50 ☐
Summer Camp at Trebizon   £1.50 ☐
Into the Fourth at Trebizon   £1.25 ☐
The Hockey Term at Trebizon   £1.50 ☐
The Big Swim of the Summer   60p   ☐
A Horse Called September   £1.50 ☐
Me, Jill Robinson and the Television Quiz   £1.25 ☐
Me, Jill Robinson and the Seaside Mystery   £1.25 ☐
Me, Jill Robinson and the Christmas Pantomime   £1.25 ☐
Me, Jill Robinson and the School Camp Adventure   £1.25 ☐

Elyne Mitchell
Silver Brumby's Kingdom   85p ☐
Silver Brumbies of the South   95p ☐
Silver Brumby   85p ☐
Silver Brumby's Daughter   85p ☐
Silver Brumby Whirlwind   50p ☐

Mary O'Hara
My Friend Flicka Part One   85p ☐
My Friend Flicka Part Two   60p ☐

To order direct from the publisher just tick the titles you want
and fill in the order form.   **D8**

All these books are available at your local bookshop or newsagent, or can be ordered direct from the publisher.

To order direct from the publishers just tick the titles you want and fill in the form below.

Name _____

Address _____

_____

Send to:
Dragon Cash Sales
PO Box 11, Falmouth, Cornwall TR10 9EN.

Please enclose remittance to the value of the cover price plus:

UK 45p for the first book, 20p for the second book plus 14p per copy for each additional book ordered to a maximum charge of £1.63.

BFPO and Eire 45p for the first book, 20p for the second book plus 14p per copy for the next 7 books, thereafter 8p per book.

Overseas 75p for the first book and 21p for each additional book.

Dragon Books reserve the right to show new retail prices on covers, which may differ from those previously advertised in the text or elsewhere.